The Magical Garden of Lucinda Mae

HALEY JEAN

Copyright © 2023 Haley Jean

Cover design by Tom Elmendorf

All rights reserved. No part of this publication may be reproduced, stored or transmitted in any form or by any means, electronic, mechanical, photocopying, recording, scanning, or otherwise without written permission from the publisher. It is illegal to copy this book, post it to a website, or distribute it by any other means without permission.

This book is a work of fiction. Names, characters, places, and incidents are the product of the author's imagination or are used fictionally. Any resemblance to actual events, locales, or persons, living or dead, is coincidental.

First edition

ISBN: 979-8-218-30370-9

CONTENTS

The Great Upheaval	1
Cale Cove	9
Suddenly Gone	18
Wildflowers and Weeds	21
Moving on and Moving Forward	30
The Locket	36
Bittersweet	40
Still Here	45
Never Left	52
Lost Connection	57
Back to Reality	70
Painting Outside the Lines	76
All Good Things Come to an End	85
Spilling the Tea	88
Three's a Crowd	94
Miles Meets the Garden	100
Pond Plans Planted	105
The Carnival	115
Apologies	125
Aftermath	129
Where There's a Will There's a Way	137
Louie's Jaunt	142

Flame or Fortune	147
When the Night is Over	153
Rebirth	156
It Goes On	162
Patty's Lemon Cookies	
Patty's Mint Tea	
Acknowledgements	

To all of the hearts broken through grief and expanded through love: from your pain may you sprout beauty.

1

THE GREAT UPHEAVAL

Mae, 2022

"Your position has been eliminated." Though it happened a week ago, Mae was still replaying the conversation in her head, lying on the couch, one leg and one arm draped off, attempting to create space between limbs in the unbearable spring heat—it was one of those freak midwestern days in the 90s that belongs in July but sometimes peeks its curious head in May.

Eight years she gave them. Eight years of fighting downtown traffic, exchanging pleasantries with strangers in the elevator, drinking burnt office coffee, even sacrificing her personal comfort by wearing a real bra every day! For what? Eliminated. Cast away just like the discarded post-its of her creative ideas falling on deaf ears in the weekly team meetings. Eight years of sitting in a cubicle for ten hours a day, thinking she was building toward some sort of a career, just to be cast away and her job outsourced to a contractor without a second thought.

Perhaps the most egregious offense was eight years of dealing with a narcissistic boss, Angie. Mae still shuddered at the thought of the "click, click, click" of Angie's impossibly high heels approaching Mae's cubicle, surrounded by the sickeningly sweet cloud of perfume and neurosis that preceded her entrance. If Mae was being honest with herself, she was burnt out and embittered from the corporate world. And now she was a dejected pancake, slowly melting into the furniture. Mae allowed her mind to wander to the night that occurred after she got laid off, the night she also left her boyfriend.

Mae hadn't intended to end her year-long relationship with Jared, a personal injury attorney she met on the elevator of her office building. Things had been going well. Lukewarm, but steady. That is, up until the day she was laid off, which happened to be Jared's birthday. They had planned to have dinner with his parents at some swanky supper club that evening. When Mae called him beforehand to tell him of her awful day at work, she pleaded with him, "Please, *pleeeease* don't mention this to your parents. I'm embarrassed and don't want to talk about it with them. I want to keep today focused on you."

He had been seemingly understanding, replying with, "Yeah, of course, babe. Don't mention it." So, when they were five minutes into their brandy old fashioneds at Mr. T's Steakhouse later that night, Mae struggled to hide her surprise when Jared's father, Chip, leaned into her and muttered, "Hey, don't let it get you down, kid. You won't need a job with Jared anyway." Chip followed up his aside with a wink, making Mae's skin crawl and cheeks flush with discomfort.

"Jared…" Mae gave him a sharp look.

"Oh, right. I mentioned it to my dad on the way here. It's no biggie, Mae, really. Once we're married and I make partner, you'll be too busy helping Ma plan the firm's social events to even think about drawing pictures on the computer." At this, Chip clinked Jared's glass in a *cheers* as they laughed and Jared's threateningly thin mother, Janet, swirled her martini, looking around the bar, bored.

Mae couldn't believe what she was hearing. She and Jared had never even talked about marriage, much less her becoming his firm's social chair. And she did not "draw pictures on the computer." She was a graphic designer and a good one at that. How much more condescending could Jared be? Mae clenched her jaw and forced her lips into a fake smile, choosing to keep the peace for birthday's sake and revisit the conversation later.

On the way home, Mae sat in the passenger seat, nervously smoothing her dress as she decided to broach the subject. "Hey, I really didn't appreciate you telling your parents about my layoff after I told you not to."

"Aw, Mae, c'mon. You're too sensitive. I promise they don't care. And neither do I. You're too cute to be stuck doing the whole career thing anyway." Jared reached across the console and gathered Mae's hand in his, kissing her fingers. Mae always fell for his cute gestures like this but tonight it wasn't hitting the same.

"Career thing? Jared, I spent eight years there. I worked really hard, and I cared a lot about that job. It's not just something to throw away."

"Yeah, but you don't want to be doing that forever, right? You're meant to be on my arm, my perfect little complement." His pleading grin and searching eyes looked for confirmation in hers.

"Hell no, Jared! Where did you get this idea that my job was a layover on the way to being your trophy wife? We've never even discussed marriage and now I'm locked into indentured servitude?! Pull the car over." Mae was fuming.

Grin now gone, Jared flared his nostrils, and to Mae's surprise, he actually pulled the car over. "Look. I haven't known when the right time to bring this up was, but I didn't like you working there anyway. Putting on your pencil skirts and heels every day and guys looking at you. You'd be much better suited to stay at home and run our life than be in an office."

"I can't actually believe we're having this conversation right now." Mae was dumbstruck. Had Jared shown tendencies toward douchebaggery in the past? Of course. He's a personal injury attorney, and Mae knew that job came with a prerequisite of equal parts arrogance and self-unawareness. But to this extreme?

"Jared, we're done." Mae said, smiling incredulously. "I want no part of this future you've envisioned for us, and I honestly want no part of the rest of this ride home together." Mae opened the car door and stepped out. Closing the door behind her, she began to walk home.

Jared rolled the window down as he drove beside her. "One day you're gonna realize what you lost here. You'll figure it out when I have someone younger, hotter, and thinner." Jared slammed on the accelerator, and as Mae watched the black Mercedes fade into the distance, she felt not sadness, not regret, but relief.

Lying on the couch now, Mae recounted that night, as she had every day since it happened, and thought of what her grandmother, Lucy, used to say, "Some days you're the windshield; some days you're the bug." In this situation, Mae was sure it was possible to be both. Grandma Lucy passed nearly three years ago, but lately Mae's heart ached with the fresh wound of losing the one person in the world who truly understood her. What would she think of Mae now? Boyfriendless, jobless, collecting boob sweat in a ratty t-shirt on her sofa.

Lucinda Mae came from a line of seven Lucindas, each one going by their middle name, except her grandmother that is. Lucinda Antoinette did everything to the beat of her own drum, choosing her first name included. Much to the dismay of her mother, Lucinda Rose, she shortened hers to Lucy instead. Mae never knew whether it was because her grandmother didn't identify with Antoinette or because she never did anything she didn't want to, but Mae loved her a little bit more because of it.

Mae peeled herself from the faux leather couch and retrieved a shoe box from her closet shelf. Elegantly decoupaged with floral scrapbooking paper and flowers she'd dried and pressed herself, the box stored handwritten short stories that Lucy penned in the later years of her life. Despite her free spirit and hunger for adventure, Lucy lived the expected American dream as a stay-at-home wife of a beloved community pastor, and then mother of six children. Once the children were grown and she had the time and capacity to hold more than seven schedules in her brain, she signed up for a creative writing class at the community college. Mae thought it was brave that her grandma never gave up on her dream of writing.

Lucy wrote the most captivating short stories Mae had ever read. Stories of love and loss, but most entrancing, were the stories of the characters' connection with the natural world. The way Lucy painted the picture of humans and spirits made it feel as if the natural and spirit worlds were as close as words on the reverse side of a book's page, one juxtaposed to another, an organic continuation. Mae had always marveled at Lucy's observation of even the tiniest creatures in the world, teaching Mae as a child to revere all life, for it was no more and no less than human life. Mae grew up collecting feathers, bird nests, and rocks, knowing that another sentient being once valued them as she did made her feel at one with all that is.

Grandma Lucy was Mae's biggest cheerleader and encouraged her creativity long after she'd abandoned it in middle school, after the countless "You can't make a living doing that" comments had taken the wind out of Mae's sails. Mae had many forms of creative expression: painting, writing, photography. Each pulled at something in the core of her being that craved unleashing. Mae kept it inside, where the potential lay in wait—always ready but never allowed to break free—all because its monetization was not easily discernible by the adults in her life.

"There's making a living and then there's making a life, baby. Don't forget to do the latter," Grandma Lucy used to say.

Mae knew Lucy wouldn't want her to wallow for one more minute because she treated life as a precious and perpetually limitless gift, bursting with potential. "What do you think, Louie? What's next for us?" Mae said.

Louie, Mae's orange tabby cat, stared back at her blankly, then licked his lips. Louie seemingly cared only about where his next fix of catnip or wheatgrass was coming from, occasionally allowing Mae a snuggle to remain in her good graces. Louie stood up from his post on the couch arm and stretched, downward-dog yoga style, then hopped over to the windowsill and sat, attentively watching the chirping birds in the oak tree beyond the window.

Mae leafed through the papers in her Grandma Lucy's memory box and a map fell out. Lucy loved maps because she loved the discovery available on road trips. She had named all six of her children after towns found on maps of places they'd explored. The map now gracing Mae's lap was a local one—nothing new to her. Yet as she looked closer, a curiosity washed over her like the first peek of sunshine on your face upon leaving the house, enveloping all the senses.

"Wait a second…" Mae said, looking closer.

Her eyes zeroed in on a town, her mouth agape. Cale Cove. "No way."

Cale Cove was a fictional—or at least Mae thought it was fictional—town in some of Grandma Lucy's stories. It was a quaint, charming community, much of what Mae expected from the storyline of a Hallmark Christmas movie. But Cale Cove wasn't real. There weren't even coves in the landlocked Midwest. Lakes, sure. But weren't coves an ocean thing?

"Mrrraaeeew," Louie articulated through another stretch.

Mae collected the papers and returned them to the floral box, placing the box back on the closet shelf. She needed to go for a walk and get some air. This was too weird. After changing clothes (rather, sliding on shorts that were not necessary to wear while alone in an apartment), Mae stepped out into the heat and started toward the bike path. When walking didn't feel fast enough, she started to jog. Mae hated the word 'jog.' It was like discounting yourself from being a runner because you were slow by someone else's standards. Mae was running. Slowly.

Mae loved the meditative clarity that running provided. The slow, steady inhale for three steps and the countering exhale. She also loved the peace that watching the vastness and deep blue, almost ocean-like presence that Lake Michigan brought to her busy mind. So, when the path split, Mae's feet carried her toward the lake path on her regular running route. Some days she stopped and watched; other days she blazed by, leaning into the full strength of her legs, pushing her potential into the path's endless miles. Today's heat caused Mae to slow to a walk, eventually stopping to gaze at the lake.

What a lot of people miss, Mae thought, was the tiny worlds alive around them, hidden in plain sight when one doesn't take the time to pause. The Lakefront Trail in Chicago was a case in point. It juxtaposed the bustling Lake Shore Drive, on which hundreds of cars whizzed by every day, hardly paying notice to the grandeur of the lake. Mae had nothing but time today, so she sat at the water's edge, folding her long legs under her, attention lost in the slippery algae-covered rocks and foamy breath of water collecting between them.

As her pulse slowed, her mind returned to the old map. Sure, this could be just a weird occurrence that Cale Cove existed in real life, but something about *when* she saw it on the map—her life circumstances of newfound singledom in work and romance, along with missing Lucy—made it feel synchronous. Watching the water washed in and out by waves gracefully below, Mae thought, "What if I went there? What if I went to Cale Cove?"

She posed this question to her mother on the phone later that night.

"Cale Cove? Honey, that's just a storybook town Grandma made up." Mae could tell her mom was distracted, the sounds of clanging pots and running water filled the background as her mother cooked dinner. She could picture her pinching the phone between her ear and shoulder, a habit Mae herself had picked up from her gregarious mother.

"But it's not, mom! It's on the map that was stuck in between her stories. It literally fell into my lap like I was supposed to see it. I want to go. I think I need to." How had no one in her family heard of this place?

"You sure you're not seeing something where there's nothing because you've been through a lot the past few weeks, Mae? Maybe you need to think this through more," Mae's mom replied.

"I don't think I do. I was careful and deliberate with Jared and that was a waste. I was steady and calculated with my career and that ended. Maybe I just need to go with it and see what happens. At worst, it's a colossal failure and I just end up back with you and dad," Mae laughed at the possibility, received by only the sound of a stovetop sizzle at the other end. "Mom, I'm joking. I'm like Louie, I always land on my feet."

"Louie lands on his belly."

"OK, fair. But I'm going to Cale Cove."

"I support you with whatever you want to do Mae. You've got a good head on your shoulders," Mae's mother said over the sounds of stir-frying meat, "but you can't just do this millennial thing and gallivant around without ever getting a real career or keeping a boyfriend or making me some grandbabies. My clock is ticking too, little miss."

"Ugh. I'm hanging up now." Mae promptly tapped the end call button with an eye roll so big she wondered if her eyeballs would be stuck in her skull like that forever.

2

CALE COVE

Mae, 2022

The perk of having a slimy landlord is that they rarely want your agreement in writing. Chad, Mae's landlord, had allowed Mae to lease the apartment initially because he'd just lost a tenant suddenly and didn't want to be out the rent money for any gap of time. Mae was fresh out of college with no rental history, no credit history, and was making scant enough to cover all of the necessities every month, so Chad's willingness to accept her tenancy seemed like a gift from above. She'd never considered that having no legal recourse, such as a signed rental agreement, would backfire when maintenance issues arose, which they had frequently over the past several months.

    Now, however, she would see the reward of her risky arrangement repay her handsomely when she informed Chad that she would be moving out with zero notice. Mae drafted a letter informing him of her departure and dropped it in his mailbox before driving her small, jam-packed SUV out of town. Pulling away from the apartment and city she spent years making feel like home didn't feel sad to her. It felt more like the kind of ending to a TV show that's well-timed: the chapter closed, loose ends tied up, this part of the story finished. With the window cracked and breeze combing her hair, she let the sense of complete freedom take over and a genuinely carefree smile spread across her face.

A few hours later, Mae arrived in Cale Cove, greeted by a small green roadside sign that informed her the population was 5,467 and she was certifiably insane to come here on a whim with not so much as a plan for where to sleep. OK, the second part was her own projection, not actually printed on the population sign.

Mae drove down Main Street, taking in the town. Boutiques, salons, bars, and other businesses surrounded a large green space, in the center of which a gazebo stood. Yoga mats sprawled the floor of the gazebo as a group of women upon them moved through a sun salutation. Throughout the park stood majestic oak trees providing shade for the children running beneath them. The town was every bit as quaint and movie-like as Lucy's stories led Mae to imagine.

Driving past the main square of downtown, the street turned residential, trading mom-and-pop shops for beautiful old homes, some restored and some in need of repair. Mae muttered to herself, "Alright Lucy, you lured me here. Now help me figure out where to…" As soon as she spoke the words, her eyes spotted a bright red "for rent" sign in front of a charming navy-blue bungalow. "…stay."

"No freaking way! How's that for luck, Louie?" Louie opened one eye from his nap in the front seat and stretched one paw forward before going back to sleep.

She pulled her car into the driveway and walked up to the door. Just as she lifted her hand to knock, she heard a voice, "Nobody's home, honey!"

Mae looked around and spotted an elderly woman rocking on the porch next door. "I'm sorry?"

"Miles. He runs the coffee shop in town—Cove Coffee. If you're looking to speak to him about renting, you'll find him there during the day," the stranger said.

"How did you...?"

"Know you were looking to rent?" The stranger leaned back in her chair, laughing to herself, then sipped from her mug. "I know everyone here, but I don't know you. I assumed you must be new and looking for a place to stay," she explained, nodding toward Mae's car, packed to the brim with her belongings obscuring all the windows.

"Ah yes, I suppose that's a giveaway," Mae said through a grin. The warmth of the stranger's face made Mae feel at home already. "Thanks so much."

Mae recalled passing Cove Coffee on the way into town, remembering it was just down the block and around the corner. After cracking a window for Louie, she decided to walk. It felt good to stretch her legs after driving and the sun on her face was a delightful welcome to her new town. Mae pulled her hair into a ponytail as she rounded the corner to Cove Coffee. Once there, she pushed open the door and the charming bell that hung from it chimed. The gentle smell of fresh ground coffee enveloped her senses.

"Wow. That smells amazing," she muttered to herself.

"Thank you much; trying out a new blend today." Mae jumped at the sound of a voice behind the counter. She was so lost in the scent, she nearly missed the man stocking sugar packets, which was an impressive feat, given he stood at least six feet tall with a wide, white, welcoming smile that lit up the room. His hazel eyes watched her in amusement as she looked around, marveling at the antique coffee grinders hanging on display around the seating area. Cove Coffee had everything Mae loved about coffee shops: a fireplace, big plush chairs in which to lose yourself with a good book, smooth jazz playing softly in the background, a gentle din of conversation, and keys tapping on laptops.

"You must be Miles," said Mae, hoping against all hope that the flush of her cheeks looked to be from her walk there more than the effect of noticing him noticing her. Her caramel brown eyes and long, dark hair were striking, such that she rarely wore makeup to avoid unnecessarily drawing more attention to herself. Miles averted his eyes to the menu on the bar and pushed it toward Mae.

"That I am. What can I get for you?" Miles said, as Mae eyed the menu.

"Unfortunately, I'm already heavily caffeinated so I should probably steer clear of that tempting blend…" Mae said contemplatively.

"Well, that's just a shame. It's my favorite one yet. Added in a little nutmeg while it brewed and it is just," Miles mimed a chef's kiss in reply. "I suppose you'll just have to come back for it," Miles said, smiling coyly.

"This could be a regular stop for me if I lived just up the street," Mae replied, eyes still wandering through the cafe, "which is actually what I came here for. Your neighbor told me it's your blue house with the 'for rent' sign?"

"Yes, I actually just put that sign out today. It's a family friend's house that I helped renovate but they're not sure they want to sell quite yet. I'm not sure how long they'll want to rent it before selling, but that's a definite possibility—just something you should know if you're interested," Miles explained. "I can grab you the rental agreement to look over while you sip…?" Miles's eyes waited for Mae's direction.

"A lavender mint iced tea please. And yes, that would be awesome." A written rental agreement? Already an improvement. Just a half hour later, Mae left the coffee shop with a new place to live. It took a quick few hours to move in, unpack, and settle Mae's few belongings, which fit well alongside the furniture that the house provided. Mae lay down for a nap on the cozy memory foam bed and quickly slipped into a deep sleep. Dreams came quickly and incoherently. The last thing Mae remembered before waking was seeing her grandmother Lucy's face, one of her chocolate-brown eyes obscured by a devious wink, followed by a knowing laugh. Mae awoke, missing the familiar face, framed by her gray-streaked wild and curly dark hair, crooked smile spread across her face.

Mae turned over and checked the time on her phone. She slept less than an hour but felt refreshed. After answering a few texts to report that all was well and she was settled in Cale Cove, Mae decided to walk downtown to find some dinner. The hot spring day had her desiring a cold beer, so she found herself at the local brewery, The Crooked Cask. Mae loved meeting strangers; sometimes she even liked them better than people she knew, so she slid onto a barstool, looking forward to bantering with the bartender, a woman who was leaning against the tap station, absentmindedly weaving her curly mop of hair into an unruly blonde plait.

"Hey there, what can I get you?" the bartender asked.

"I would love a pint of your saison and a bacon cheeseburger with fries," Mae said, quickly eyeing the menu posted above the bar.

"Coming right up," replied the bartender, handing her a plastic number after punching the order into a tablet. She poured and placed the pint in front of Mae and carried the ticket back to the kitchen. When she returned, she eyed Mae inquisitively. "Have you been in before? I don't recognize you."

"Nope, it's my first time here. I actually just moved in up the street. Have you worked here a while?" Mae said.

"Since we opened, five years ago. It's actually my place."

"No kidding! That's awesome. What's your name?"

"I'm Cassie," the bartender replied, sticking out her hand for Mae to shake.

"Cassie. I'm Mae. It's nice to meet you," Mae said enthusiastically.

"Yeah, you, too. What brings you to our tiny town?" Cassie's bright blue eyes, framed with a thick layer of mascara, focused on Mae with genuine interest. The typical here-for-my-lake-house out-of-towners were not as open and social as Mae, so she struck Cassie as peculiar.

"Oh, it's a long, weird story," Mae hesitated.

"I'm here all night," Cassie said, leaning her palms on the bar, curious. Her stance revealed a tattoo of hops clusters and wheat tendrils wrapping from her wrist up toward her elbow.

"Well, I guess it's not that long," Mae replied, taking a sip of her beer before continuing.

"My grandma used to write short stories, fictional as far as I knew. I saved them after she died a few years ago and was just looking through them the other day when a map fell out of the pages and I saw this place, Cale Cove, on it. It's weird because I always thought Cale Cove was a fictional town in the stories she wrote. Why would she use a real place in a fictional story? I guess the strangeness of it along with being newly single and unemployed flipped a switch in me. Why not? Why not uproot my life and try something else?"

Cassie laughed. "Why not? You're a brave soul, Mae. I like that kind of gumption."

Mae laughed too. "I mean, I guess it's a little crazy and totally out of character for me. But it just feels like the next right thing, so…" she finished her sentence with a shrug and a long sip from her pint. "What about you? Did you grow up in Cale Cove?"

"I did, yeah. I'm related to like half the town so…oh sorry, one sec." Cassie turned her attention to two men walking through the door. Mae watched her interact with what she assumed were regular customers, as they greeted Cassie with fist bumps. Cassie grinned widely and her dimples showed her familiarity with the men. While she took their orders and chatted, Mae sat back and observed in the brewery. The bar area was small, situated just across from the entry door. It curved in a half horseshoe shape with the door to the kitchen at one end. Beyond that, there was a hallway that led down to a high-ceilinged room, what Mae assumed was additional seating and perhaps the brewing area. The dim lighting and warm colors of the wood bar made the whole place feel like a cozy extension of a living room—a place where you could hang out for hours and always feel welcome.

Mae noticed two other people at the opposite end of the bar—a couple, she guessed in their fifties. They were deep in conversation, unaware that she had joined the bar. They talked and laughed at each other, only breaking eye contact to dig into the massive plate of nachos in front of them. The men talking to Cassie grabbed their beer and walked down the hallway, disappearing from sight, just as the door opened again. An aloof-looking man walked in, looking as surprised as one might if they fell asleep in their bed and woke up inside of a brewery. The couple at the end of the bar as well as Cassie said in unison, "Hey Jim!"

The man flattened his pouf of windblown gray hair while looking around the bar, "Well, hey everybody!" A bright smile quickly emerged on his face, revealing a gilded molar. He leaned the walking sticks he was carrying against the wall and approached the bar.

Cassie directed her gaze to Mae and said, "Mae, this is Jim, the nicest guy in town." Then, looking at him, "Jim, this is Mae. She's new in town so be nice," she said in jest.

"Mae. That's a name I've never heard before," Jim stuck out his hand and Mae shook it, but Jim paused for a moment, "I...probably won't remember it." His hands were as soft as the apology in his eyes, searching hers over the rim of his glasses sliding down the bridge of his nose.

"That's OK!" Mae replied. "It's hard to remember new names." Jim nodded in agreement, looking slightly lost. He wandered down to the couple at the end of the bar and engaged them in conversation, placing a hand on each of their backs.

"I'll tell you more about him later," Cassie said to Mae with a wink.

Mae's dinner arrived in a few minutes, and after enjoying the mouth-watering burger, she asked Cassie for another pint. There was something about Cassie that Mae liked, even trusted right away. She was hoping this would be her first Cale Cove friend.

After pouring another for Mae, Cassie started, "So Jim. He's not shy about people knowing, so I thought I'd fill you in. He got into a freak bike accident a few years back. Was riding on the trail that goes through town after a thunderstorm and a broken tree limb fell on him, knocking him out cold. He suffered brain damage and has a pretty limited short-term memory now. That's why he said he'll have a hard time remembering your name. He can make new memories, but it takes much longer now. But he's likely the happiest guy you'll meet because of it. He's living in the moment, always totally happy to be doing what he's doing, and most of the time that's just walking around town. He'll stop into the businesses, and everyone loves him."

"Oh wow. That's crazy," Mae contemplated, trying to imagine how your life would change without short-term memory.

"He always says he doesn't want people to feel bad for him, so don't. I see that look you're making."

Mae corrected her face back to neutrality. "Sorry, it's just. I can't even imagine…"

"I know, right? Hang out in here long enough and you'll get to know a lot of the regulars. All unique and beautiful stories. That's why I love owning my own place here on Main St. The people."

"Very cool, Cassie. You've got a nice place here." They chatted some more and then Mae closed out her tab, bid Cassie goodbye, and pushed open the door to the warm evening outside, worn from the day. As she walked home, she noticed the aged buildings of downtown, all of them a different character of brick and stained glass, many adorned with planters bursting with green life and brightly colored flowers. An ivy leaf graced her forehead as she passed under a hanging basket, gently tickling her hairline. As her feet carried her past a sports bar, she saw Jim through the window, standing at the bar with his arms around two other patrons. As he turned and made eye contact with Mae, his face lit up and he waved excitedly. Mae smiled and waved back, though she didn't stop walking. She smiled to herself, already feeling a little bit at home in this little mysterious town.

As she lay in bed that night, Mae thought about Jim losing his memory, wondering if it would be like losing a part of yourself. And about Cassie, wondering about her family legacy in Cale Cove. And about Miles, trying not to wonder about him. She again fell into a deep sleep with a flurry of dreams filled with faces she didn't know but that felt familiar. Everyone was trying to talk to her, but she couldn't hear them, like she was wearing earplugs. Faces surrounding her in all directions with kind but urgent requests for her attention, splitting her focus in multiple directions. Mae felt flustered at not being able to help them, and suddenly Lucy appeared again with a mischievous smile and wink. Mae awoke briefly, remembering only Lucy's face, then fell back asleep.

3

SUDDENLY GONE

Lucy, 1956

"Come help me with dinner" said a stern but soft, clearly exhausted voice.

Lucy was on her back, atop the blankets of her bed, hot tears streaming down her face, pooling in her ears. She swallowed the lump of loss in her throat, forcing down the sadness that threatened to drown her. Her mother, Lucinda Rose, stood at the doorway of her bedroom, arms crossed in impatience, stoic in the grief that crumbled Lucy's heart.

"I can't momma. I can't." Lucy muttered between shaky breaths. She rolled to her side, pulling her knees into her chest in fetal position, as if decreasing her physical body's footprint could decrease the heaviness of loss seeping through her bones. She longed for her mother to comfort her. To sit on the edge of her bed and rub her back like she did when Lucy was young. But she wasn't young anymore. Seventeen now, Lucy was a girl on the verge of adulthood, and her mother somehow interpreted this as evidence of how Lucy was now misbehaving, unable to hide her unruly emotions as well as her mother could.

"What you've lost is nothing compared to what I've lost. We must pick up and move on. You will help me with dinner now, Antoinette," Rose used her daughter's formal name, despite her constant pleas to use her childhood nickname of Lucy. The one he used.

It had been one week since Lucy's father and Rose's husband had passed away suddenly. A professional home builder, John had reported to work that day like any other, set to work on installing insulation in a new home under construction. When his crew left for lunch, he told himself he'd get just a bit more work done before taking a break of his own. Those few extra minutes made the difference of a literal lifetime when his boot caught on the rung of a ladder he was climbing, and he fell twelve feet onto his back. The coroner said he died on impact, and Mae thought she might too after the police officer broke the news to their family that evening.

The next week was a blur of neighbors, family, and church members bringing casseroles, hugs, tissues, and unending presence to Lucy's family. The funeral came and went; she couldn't tell you who was there if she tried. John was Lucy's best friend in the world, the only one who never imposed a timeline of marriage, children, and homemaking on her. He brought her fishing on Lake Cale in the wee hours of the balmy summer mornings, evading her mother's watchful eye, but always got Lucy back in time to clean up for school, freshly prepared for her math tests for which he loved quizzing her. Without her father, Lucy didn't know who she would tell her dreams to. Who would dare to believe she could be more than a housewife?

Rose left Lucy's doorway, and after expending a herculean effort to lift herself off the bed, Lucy padded to the kitchen where she found her mother hastily chopping vegetables for a stew. Rose's hair was tied neatly in a bun, her apron properly tied over her dress, just as it always had been. Before or after tragedy, Rose's appearance would never tell. A small wood stove crackled in the corner, and Lucy could already smell bread baking in the oven. The warm swell of the scent nearly brought Lucy to tears again. Stew with bread was her father's favorite dinner after the long days spent building in yet-to-be-heated homes.

    Lucy joined her mother at the stove and joined the dance of preparing dinner beside her, a carefully coordinated waltz they'd honed over time, always knowing where the other was and accommodating each other's movements in the modest kitchen. Lucy loved her mother, of course, but couldn't understand why she was indignant toward Lucy's reaction to her father's death. If they could just share in it, hold each other through the stabbing pain of losing someone so dear to them both, maybe, just maybe they could make it through. Lucy glanced at her mother sideways and studied her stern face; it was completely devoid of emotion. Lucy never felt further away from her than standing next to her right now, their shared yet unspoken grief digging an insurmountable canyon between the women.

4

WILDFLOWERS AND WEEDS

Mae, 2022

The next morning, Mae awoke and realized she never bought any groceries. Slipping on a pair of shorts, zipping up a hoodie, and pulling her hair back into a loose braid, she headed to Cove Coffee. Miles looked up from a book he was reading as the door chimed and smiled politely.

"Good morning to Cale Cove's newest resident. How was your first night in the house? Nothing spooky I hope."

Mae opened her mouth to return a morning greeting but paused, mouth ajar at Miles' suggestion. She raised an eyebrow and said, "Spooky? I slept like a baby. You didn't tell me the place was haunted."

"Ah, it's not. I'm only kidding. You know how people get about old houses—assuming there's something supernatural going on. What can I get you today?"

Mae had a feeling Miles wasn't completely kidding, but she also didn't know how to press the subject, so instead she said, "I would love a cup of that divine smelling blend you had yesterday and a bagel sandwich please." Breakfast was Mae's favorite meal.

"Of course. Take a seat and I'll bring it out in a minute." Miles replaced his thumb for a bookmark to keep his page then disappeared into the kitchen to get to work on Mae's breakfast. The door chimed behind her, ushering in Jim, looking windswept and slightly lost again.

"Oh, hey Jim. Long time no see," Mae greeted him.

"Hey…" Jim contemplated, "you know my name?" cocking his head to the side, wire-rimmed glasses slipping farther down his nose.

Mae smiled patiently, "Of course! Remember we met last night at The Crooked Cask? Cassie introduced us."

"Oh, that's right! I told you I wouldn't remember your name," Jim chuckled to himself, his eyes pleading forgiveness from Mae.

"Ah, nothing on it. Would you like to join me for breakfast? I've just ordered and was about to take a seat."

"Would I?!" Jim's face split into a radiant grin, like someone just told him he'd won the lottery. Cassie was right. He certainly seemed like the happiest guy in town.

Jim and Mae settled at a table by the window and their orders arrived a minute later.

"I see you've wasted no time making friends with the Cove's finest," Miles noted as he put the plates on the table.

Though Mae was sure Miles directed the observation to her, Jim replied, "I know! I'm a lucky man today." Mae blushed and Miles said nothing further, smirking as he walked away.

Mae sipped the coffee blend that Miles was proudly brewing when they first met. She felt a part of her soul melt into the cup with the first sip. She inhaled the coffee, pulling the mug close to her face and letting her eyes close for a moment. Was that really just yesterday? How could a place feel like home after less than 24 hours? Mae and Jim ate in silence, casually people watching the passersby outside. After several minutes, Jim turned to her and said in a serious tone, "Sometimes I wonder where people are always going."

"What do you mean? I'm sure they're going to work or errands or whatever," Mae replied.

"Walking so quickly, heads down, most times on their phones. I think a lot of people don't even know what season it is because they're hustling their way through life, one task at a time. It's a shame, you know? Life's right now."

"So true," Mae agreed, toasting her mug to Jim's.

Mae spent the rest of breakfast marveling at the wisdom Jim didn't seem to know he possessed. Afterward, Mae walked home, changed into her running clothes, and headed out on foot toward the crushed limestone trail that snaked its way through town. Her favorite way to explore new places was on foot, and after a half mile she picked up the pace into a steady run. Once on the trail, she followed its bends through a wooded paradise that smelled of fallen pine needles. Running had been Mae's sanity through heartbreaks, the sadness of saying goodbye to Lucy, job stress, and so much more. Something about pushing her body to do difficult things while working through difficult emotions in unison made everything feel more doable. It was hard, but she was here, doing it, getting through it.

Running was also there to clear her busy mind or allow a space for it to run wild, processing whatever it needed to process. On this particular run, as Mae breathed in the scent of the surrounding nature, her mind wandered to the dream she had the night before, the faces that needed to speak to her, but she couldn't hear them. Who were they? Why did they look familiar yet no one she knew in her waking life? And what did they have to do with Lucy? Mae dreamt of Lucy often in the months that followed her death, and she always took comfort in seeing her smiling face, deep chocolate brown eyes nestled in the narrow slits that hugged them beneath crow's feet. She'd not dreamt of other people with Lucy before though. And for some reason, that struck Mae as peculiar.

Mae let her feet lead her to the bridge that connected the path over a narrow section of Lake Cale, slowing and pausing to a stop on the bridge, allowing her to look out at the lake. The absence of a breeze today made the glasslike water serenely still, save for a few ducks paddling by. Mae's attention turned to the edge of the shore when she heard a prehistoric-sounding cry. Two sandhill cranes stood in the shallow water, surrounded by tall wispy grass, staring directly at her. Mae stared back, studying their tall, slender bodies, noticing the spot of red plumage around their eyes. Several moments passed before she realized they were watching her in return.

    She turned behind her and swept the area with her gaze, but she was still alone. The cranes remained statuesque, refusing to tear their watchful eyes from her. Never a fan of being the center of attention, Mae turned and began running again, down the dusty path, through a canopy of trees that shrouded the trail, taking the first fork after the bridge, rounding the streets of downtown toward her new abode. Slowing to walk when she reached home, Mae pulled her headphones out of her ears, hearing a friendly, "Hey there, neighbor!"

    The elderly woman who had helped her find Miles was on her porch again, rocking in a white wicker chair and sipping from an oversized mug cupped between her knobby, sun-spotted hands. The woman's demeanor was unrushed and placid, as if she had all the time in the world to do exactly what she was doing. Her age wasn't given away by the lines on her forehead like most people, but by the ones hugging her grin and surrounding her welcoming eyes, as if her face had spent all of her days in a pleasant smile. The woman's lucent tranquility made Mae, one of anxious mind and perpetual mental lists, uncomfortable. Mae climbed her porch steps and smiled politely at the neighbor, waving. "Good morning," she hesitated, "um, sorry I don't think I got your name before?"

    "Patty…Patricia. You can call me Patty though. Or the Cookie Lady, as the kids around here do." Patty threw her head back in laughter, coinciding with the rhythm of her rock in the chair. Mae couldn't help but smile along with her; this woman radiated pure joy, made more angelic by the mane of white hair held loosely on top of her head with a claw clip.

"The Cookie Lady?" Mae smirked. "Sounds like you've done some good deeds to earn that title."

"I just love to bake. After Earl, my husband, passed, I couldn't possibly eat all these cookies on my own. So, I started bringing them out on the porch for my afternoon tea." She paused to raise her mug. "First it was one or two kids after school, but now it's dozens." Patty smiled wide, pleased with herself. "It's the highlight of my days."

"That sounds really lovely," Mae replied, genuinely intrigued by her. What a nice woman to have as a neighbor. "Have a good one, Patty." Mae ducked into the house, looking forward to a warm shower, but as she walked to the back of the house toward the stairs, her eyes couldn't help but be drawn to the backyard, an unkempt patch of green space beyond the large windows. It occurred to her that she'd never actually looked at it yesterday before renting the house. In all honesty, Mae didn't care if the place had a yard; she only needed the basics.

Instead of going upstairs to the shower, Mae found herself taking the side door to the modest back patio. She sat on the edge where the patio meets the grass and removed her shoes and socks, then looked around and, after feeling safe in the privacy of the relatively secluded yard, peeled off her sweaty tank too. The sun was creeping up to its hottest angle and she could use a tan. Mae stood for a moment in just her shorts and sports bra, and closed her eyes to soak in the moment, feeling the cool blades of grass between her toes. Opening her eyes, she took in the yard at a closer distance.

The patio was a square concrete area just beyond a sliding glass door in the back of the house. A grill was situated off to the side, along with a small wrought iron bistro table and pair of chairs. The patio was nearly surrounded by lilac bushes, offering fragrant privacy, with the exception of a small path that Mae now saw was actually half-buried bricks leading out to the rest of the yard. The bricks sat flush with the grass, the blades of which were creeping over them, wishing to reclaim them into the earth. Mae followed the path, brick by brick, to an ivy-covered archway, ushering her into what lay beyond, which, Mae assumed, was a garden.

At first glance, the overgrown patch of earth showed no evidence of ever being tended to in any kind of garden-like manner. Other than the stone fence that surrounded the unruly green space, nothing appeared to be placed there intentionally. After living in a downtown walk-up apartment for the past eight years, Mae knew close to nothing about gardening, but something about the untouched potential of this lush-yet-overgrown canvas intrigued Mae's inner green thumb. What she did know about gardening was the assault her mother led on her own flower beds' weeds every spring and throughout the summer, so Mae knew a thistle when she saw one. She began pulling at the stubborn weeds until it became apparent that she would need gloves for the task. She wrapped her fingers around and tugged at one more, but the spike dragged the flesh of her thumb and she shouted, "Damnit!" Crimson blood began to bead from her thumb as she gritted her teeth.

"You'll want to use these."

Mae spun around to the familiar voice. When she saw Miles standing there with gardening gloves in his outstretched hand, she didn't hide her surprise.

"Shit, Miles, you scared me," Mae said, wiping away a bead of forehead sweat onto the back of her hand and crossing her arms over her body, suddenly reminded she'd ditched her sweaty shirt.

"I think the thistle did that first, but I apologize. I realized I never told you where I keep the old gardening tools, in case inspiration strikes." A coy smile found its way across his face as he still offered the gloves to Mae. Mae accepted them, eyeing him suspiciously.

"And do you regularly just drop in on tenants unannounced?"

Miles laughed nervously, his eyes suddenly interested in the ground, "No, I do not. Buster needed a lunch walk so I was in the neighborhood." He nervously combed his fingers through his thick hair and looked around, anywhere but at Mae. "I just dropped him back home when I saw you ducking back into the garden, so I grabbed the gloves from the shed and met you."

"Buster?" Mae asked.

"Your neighbor Patty's dog," Miles replied, gesturing to Patty's house. "She can't get around as much as she used to, so I walk Buster for her over lunch." Miles became aware of how he might have creeped out Mae as he was explaining himself. He suddenly became self-conscious and wanted to go, to undo the entire interaction. Miles threw his hands up in front of him and backed away slowly in surrender. "That wasn't cool, you're right. I should have respected your space and not dropped by unannounced. I forgot you're not really into the fold of everybody-in-everybody's-small-town-business yet." He smiled apologetically.

He was right, Mae was caught off guard by his visit, but she could tell he was genuinely regretful. "Don't worry about it. Thanks for these," she said, holding up the gloves, then quickly added, "How much do you know about gardening?"

"Ha! Do you see the state of this place?" Miles asked rhetorically. "Clearly nothing."

"Ah alright, well I better get to it if I want to make it look like something other than a thistle propagation station." Miles nodded and left with a timid wave. Mae almost wished he'd stay.

She returned to the wannabe garden and pulled weeds for two hours before the muscles in her lower back started aching and her nose caught a whiff of her desperate need for a shower. After getting cleaned up, Mae made a list and headed to Cove's Cart, the local grocery store. Why was everything named so cutesy around here?

After collecting the necessary items in her cart and unloading them on the checkout conveyor, Mae's eyes wandered to the seedy gossip magazines and newspapers displayed beside the candy in the checkout lane. Gossip magazines were good for one location only as far as Mae was concerned, and that was the nail salon, where she could indulge in two completely unnecessary trivialities simultaneously—reshaping and painting her neglected nails and discovering the latest on Leo DiCaprio's love life—both of which happened only a few times per year.

 This time though, Mae's eyes were not distracted by the plunging satin gown and phenomenal décolletage of Leo's latest tryst but rather the booklet racked above it, *Midwest Flowers: Wild and Tame*. The cover displayed a picture of beautifully understated tiny purple flowers, green spiky things, and one that Mae did recognize—zinnias. She removed the book from its perch and after a few seconds of thumbing through, dropped it on the conveyor to join the rest of her items.

 Mae focused her attention on the cashier, making small talk as she scanned the items and placed them carefully into Mae's reusable bags. When conversation lulled, Mae turned to her wallet, retrieving the credit card from its slot, just as a deep voice brought her attention back upward.

 "Flowers, eh?" the voice said in midwestern slang as the cashier slid the final item through to the recognized ding of the barcode scanner. Mae's eyes traveled up and met with Miles' once again, laughing nervously as he stood in line behind her.

 "Yeah, I guess I thought I'd start somewhere with figuring out what I've got on my hands," she paused, then offered, "impulse purchase," with a shrug.

 "My last impulse purchase was a dog sweater at 2 a.m., so I'd say this is much more productive," Miles said with a timid smile. Mae wondered if he still felt bad about the garden encounter earlier that other day, then realized between that appearance and his attempt at conversation over flowers he knew nothing about, it was likely he was just trying to be friendly. Mae softened toward him in a way she wouldn't normally until the fourth or fifth meeting of any other man. Miles felt different. Demure, safer even. Mae regretted her forceful reproach of Miles in the garden and returned a compassionate smile.

"What kind of dog do you have?" Mae asked, hoping the question would be the conversational olive branch, smoothing over the unspoken discomfort of the prior exchange.

"Teddy's a golden retriever," Miles replied, adding, "with absolutely no use for a sweater." They both laughed.

Mae paid, collected her bags from the cashier, and returned home. Later that night, heart full of hope and fulfilled nostalgia of this place she didn't even know she missed, Mae fingered through her new flower book, promising herself she'd start in on the garden mess in the morning.

5

MOVING ON AND MOVING FORWARD

Lucy, 1957

Lucy walked along the shore of the lake, hoping the quiet morning would bring her peace. A gentle breeze combed her hair as she continued along the shoreline, taking in the vast water and hazy fog in the early dawn hours. She'd gotten into the habit of these early morning walks in the months after her father's death as a way to be alone with her thoughts, especially since Rose shut down every opportunity to talk about her husband and Lucy's dad, which is what Lucy needed most. She loved watching the stillness of the water before the world awoke, the creatures in the grass and trees the only souls stirring.

Lucy paused a moment, taking in the quiet rustle of leaves, watching a squirrel rummage for a lost treasure, then scamper away up the trunk of a mighty oak tree. She sat on a nearby bench and tilted her head in the direction of the sun, closing her eyes. It was during these moments alone while the rest of the world slept that she felt most herself. Sometimes, she would walk to the lake just to gaze out and weep, a steady stream of tears soaking her cheeks, neck, and shirt. Other days she would scream into the void. Still other days, she'd say nothing at all. No matter which emotion she brought, the lake and surrounding park would accept it, just as nature herself accepted all facets of her essence without apology or shame.

A nearby chickadee cooed its two-note call, a melody that always reminded Lucy of her father. John loved rising before the sun and would sit in his rocking chair by the window, one ankle resting on the other leg's knee, the other foot gently pushing him to rock as he sat with his eyes closed listening to the early morning birds. Lucy never understood why he would wake up only to go to his chair and return to a half-asleep state when he could just sleep in later, but her early morning lake walks made her realize the reason. It was John's definition of peace, and as she sat on the cold bench on the deserted shore, Lucy realized this was hers.

A year had melted away since John's death, and the emotional distance between Lucy and Rose was an ever-growing expanse of unspoken heartbreak. As the bright green life of summer transitioned to a crisp golden fall, Lucy thought her mother just needed time. Then as the snow fell, melted, and the first buds of spring began to emerge from their winter slumber, Lucy's grief failed to do the same. She felt the pit of loss in her stomach most days and her heart ached with not only the loss of her father and closest confidant, but also the loss of any connection with her mother.

Lucy felt that most days her mother might as well be a stranger. Every time something reminded Lucy of her father, like a redtail hawk effortlessly gliding through the winter skies or the first springtime chirp of the portly, pregnant robins, she wanted to share the memory as a way of keeping him alive, make it so his presence was still part of their everyday lives. But with each attempt at building these bridges across the ocean of grief to connect with her mother, Rose burned them down and shut her out. Lucy wondered how her mother could pick up and continue on with her upended life when nothing was the same as it was just a year ago.

This is how the walks began. Born out of both loneliness and wanting to be alone, Lucy found more companionship by herself outside than she did in the presence of others with whom she couldn't properly emote. She started walking while still in school, rising before the rest of the household and returning to make breakfast for her siblings before school. At first, Rose didn't notice Lucy's absence in the early morning hours because she stealthily snuck out and back in before the rest of the household awoke. Once she did, however, she never objected, as Lucy was still helping with her siblings.

John's death left the family strapped after the funeral costs and paying off his business expansion loan; now it was up to Rose to feed five hungry mouths and handle a mortgage on her own. Lucy could feel her mother's stress over making ends meet and knew the least she could do was help raise the children in the house, so rather than enjoy the summer after high school chasing boys with her classmates, Lucy kept up her walking routine before the morning chores at home, then went to her job as a secretary at the local newspaper. If she could alleviate the financial stress on her mother, perhaps they could again share the closeness she so desperately longed for.

Lucy was selected her senior year of school to participate in a special trial-run class for typing and she found herself naturally adept, her fingers dancing across the keys flawlessly like a classical pianist on a grand piano, faster and more accurate than all of her classmates. Her top marks caught the eye of her teacher, Mrs. Dupree, who referred her to her editor-in-chief husband, Duane Dupree, at the Cove Courier, the local newspaper. After a quick interview and aptitude test, Lucy started at the office answering phones, organizing mail, typing meeting notes and memos, and running coffee to the editors.

The work was easy, and Lucy found that she was good at it. She reveled in the buzz of the morning flurry of workers stepping off the elevator, hustling out in their freshly ironed suits, the aroma of coffee in Styrofoam cups and cigarette smoke wafting through the halls, and an ever-present low hum of typewriter dings, papers exchanging hands, and the quick clicking of shoes on linoleum with somewhere important to be. She almost didn't even mind when the slimy sports reporter, Stan, called her "sugar" every time he passed by because it meant someone had noticed her. Lucy was quickly finding a groove and her place in the world. Almost.

In the hour or so between finishing work and having to make dinner for the family, Lucy had been uncovering the overgrown patch of what used to be a flower bed behind the family's residence. When her dad was alive, he loved spending time bird watching, weeding, and cultivating vegetables there. Then when the garden was in a state that he deemed maintainable, completing "yard inspections." The garden was the envy of the neighborhood. It simultaneously provided a visual spectacle and a practical crop, yielding countless produce to be included in Rose's stews and pickled to sustain the family through the winter.

Rows of perfectly spaced plantings were identified by their neatly-written wooden stake signs as squash, kale, spinach, carrots, cucumbers, beans, tomatoes, and even mulberries, though the sandhill cranes usually had their way with those before John's green thumb could harvest them. Bordering the lush vegetable patch on all sides were immaculate perennial blooms of fragrant lilac bushes, trailing clematises, vibrant zinnias, bursting peonies, and Lucy's favorite, sunflowers. Fragrant in early spring, summer, and fall, offering the entire spectrum of color, and the company of hummingbirds, bumblebees, and butterflies, the garden was truly a feast for all of the senses.

To protect its bounty from hungry critters, John had built a sturdy stone fence around the perimeter that was nearly undetectable through the blooms that disguised its presence on either side. The entrance of Eden, as Lucy had nicknamed it, was shrouded in a trellis blanketed by a black-eyed Susan vine. The opposite end of the garden on the inside of the fence was John's most recent addition: a koi pond and cement bench. It took a lot of groveling and calculated persuasion on John and Lucy's part to convince Rose of this addition. After all, it was not wholly necessary, and Rose was nothing if not frugal and minimalist in every facet of her life—but they had done it and installed it last summer. Just a season before his passing.

    The idea to revive the garden came to Lucy on one particularly quiet morning walk. The garden was never important to her mother and especially after John's unexpected death, she had her hands full cleaning houses in the community to keep the family's finances afloat. Rose was a homemaker when her husband lived, and the quick switch and immediate pressure of producing a livable income for her and her children demanded not only her time, but her mental and physical energy, too. The very last thing she had the resolve to do at the end of the day or week was to breathe life into the garden that represented her late love, fully knowing the one she wishes she could breathe life back into would never breathe again. Though it pained her to see it go, the thought of being so intimately close yet so impossibly far from her beloved spurred her into inaction.

    Lucy knew it was too hard for her mother to take on the garden on top of everything else, though Lucy thought it a disservice to her father's memory to look out the kitchen window and see the once-beautiful retreat be reclaimed by the natural processes of the earth, gradually morphing into an overgrown, weedy, vine-covered mess. She first started by clearing a pathway to the bench so that she could sit and remember her dad. Mourn his absence. Somehow sitting in a space where he poured his heart and standing on the soil on which he spilled his literal sweat and blood made him feel like he wasn't so far away. Like perhaps he had just gone away on a trip and had forgotten to call but would surely be home soon.

    On this particular afternoon, Lucy was on her hands and knees battling a relentless weed tree—that's what her father had called them—that had rooted itself a little too deeply to be displaced by bare hands and a strong will alone. With her cotton skirt hiked up past her knees and her sleeves pushed to her elbows, Lucy widened her kneeling stance, bearing down into the earth as she pulled hard against the sprout. With forceful yank, her hands slipped off the offending plant and Lucy fell backward into the cement bench, hitting her head on the way down. Lucy lay there for several moments (minutes?) on the ground, exhausted. A throbbing pain at the base of her skull confirmed the egg forming below the skin. Sliding her fingers over the offending wound, Lucy confirmed she was not bleeding, and exhaled sharply in relief. With the sun setting on the horizon but still kissing the garden with its golden glow, Lucy heard the distant chirp of a cardinal and watched a redtail hawk gliding above; she couldn't help but feel her dad nearby. The garden was a mess but here she was, using her grief as motivation to restore it to its former glory. John would be proud.

6

THE LOCKET

Mae, 2022

It wasn't even noon, but Mae was up to her elbows in dirt, her knees covered in thorny scrapes, and her t-shirt was nearly soaked to the skin underneath in the bright mid-morning sun. She was barefooted, taking in all that the unruly garden had to offer. As far as Mae was concerned, it was the perfect Midwest summer day: clear blue sky, a warm gentle breeze, a whole day of potential ahead, and not an obligation in sight. Perhaps this unemployment thing wasn't so bad after all. Mae didn't realize how much she really needed a mental timeout and reset after all that had happened between losing her job and leaving that sad excuse for a boyfriend. If a girl couldn't find love in a city the size of Chicago, Mae had settled on loving only a cat. Looking around for him now, Mae worried when she didn't see him right away. Louie had accompanied her outside but after the initial perimeter sniff of the garden, showed no interest in it. Mae walked around and finally found him sprawled out on his back on the warm concrete patio, sunning his expansive furry belly.

 Back in her fourth-floor walk-up in Chicago, Mae had a tiny balcony that had just enough room for a chair and a potted plant. The tiny lemon tree she attempted to cultivate in the patio pot sadly died after starving for sunlight by fall, a true surprise to no one living in the Midwest. Still, it was a nice ambience while she had it, and Louie loved lying on the balcony, meowing, hissing at, and teasing the birds that stopped for a rest on her railing. The only other plant mothering experience Mae had was an indoor potted cactus she had impulsively purchased at the grocery store. The bright green of its trunk next to the burnt orange terra cotta pot made Mae feel like she had a bit of the exotic outdoors in the midst of a concrete jungle. After several years, it had unexpectedly grown to a confident three prickly feet tall and survived the move to Cale Cove. Its survival and hardiness were a true wonder, as she never spent much time trying to learn the skill of houseplant care.

Even after staying up late reading her new flower book, Mae still confidently knew nothing of gardening, but felt driven by her desire to shape something out of the blank slate of green she had at her disposal. Though Mae realized now that her blank slate was anything but blank, and she had spent the last three hours pulling out unwanted black walnut tree sprouts, thistles, and creeping Charlie from the lush green palette of what might have one day been, and what one day might again be, a garden.

A fragrant ground cover—revealed by her new grocery store flower book to be creeping phlox—led her on an hour-long scavenger hunt to find its origin. Each stem she pulled up led to a web of fingered roots spreading in every direction, each leading to a new source root. While its tiny purple flowers were pretty, Mae uprooted the majority of it in order to let the rest of the garden have space to shine in its own right. The pile of discarded overgrowth steadily grew toward the sky as she worked little by little through the wild green expanse. What else was in the garden, she did not yet know.

By the time the sun climbed straight overhead, Mae's stomach growled for sustenance, but she had just uncovered an old, cracked cement bench. Her head swirled with the novel rush of an archaeologist discovering a hidden past as she traced her finger along the moss-sprouted seam. Despite the heat of the day, the bench was cool to the touch, having been blanketed in foliage until twenty minutes prior. The bench was beautiful, or at least it had been at one point. The cement now aged and damp with mildew could stand for a good power washing, Mae thought, but the detail on the feet was impeccable. Mae pulled herself up to rest her tired body upon it and felt accomplished. The garden around her was still an untamed, sprawling green mess, but she had cleared this piece, and this piece felt like the first domino falling on a line of latent beauty.

Heading into the house to prepare lunch, Mae passed through the decrepit stone stanchion posts on either side of the lopsided gate at the entrance and noticed a black walnut shell, unopened, carefully placed on the top of each post.

"That's weird," Mae said to herself, looking around the yard. Nothing about the presence of the walnuts was weird—those were everywhere—but rather the placement of them, symmetrically set, one on each pillar.

While she spotted no human visitors, she could have sworn a squirrel sitting on its hind legs across the yard was watching her. A small chirp escaped the squirrel's mouth, and it bounded off into the wooded patch beyond the backyard. One by one, Mae picked up the walnuts and tossed them into the woods. Surely, the squirrel would have more use for the nuts than she would. After all, the garden already had too many that had taken root in the small space.

Mae made a sandwich and poured herself a glass of lemonade, bringing both out to the cement bench for a solo picnic. Something about this place reminded her of Lucy, though Lucy was a master of gardening, and her space would never be this disheveled. When Mae was a child, Lucy would pick her up from school and they'd walk back to Lucy's house where they spent time hanging out in her garden, eating chocolate chip cookies and playing "I Spy" until Mae's mother was done with work. Mae could still feel the soft crevices of Lucy's hand as she folded it securely around her own while they walked. She could still see her grandmother's blue and white gingham apron that she wore in the garden, attempting to keep her outfit neat, though it was always in vain because Lucy felt most at home covered in earth. Mae could still smell the delicate vanilla and jasmine of her grandmother's embrace, a place that always felt like home.

There was nothing specific here in this garden that reminded her of Lucy's own garden, but the casual simplicity of eating ham and cheese with the soil between her toes and broken twigs in her messy hair made her feel closer to Lucy than she had since she'd passed. As Mae finished her lunch, she let her eyes pan the garden while her mind paged through fond memories of Lucy. Losing your grandmother was a natural order of life, she knew. But somehow that fact didn't make the loss any less significant or painful.

As Mae swallowed the last bite of her sandwich, her eyes stopped on a glimmer in the far corner of the garden. She thought perhaps the flashy sun played a trick on her mind but as she stepped closer to where she saw it, she glimpsed the bright reflection again. Mae moved toward the object and pulled the vines and crispy leaves away from it, revealing a dirt-covered heart. She wrapped her fingers around it and pulled, discovering a chain attached. An intricately etched, heart-shaped locket lay in the palm of her hand.

Mae thumbed away more dirt off of it and turning it over, discovered the letters LAM engraved on the reverse side. Upon opening it, Mae was disappointed to see there were no pictures, but only fiber fragments of pictures long eroded. She wondered how long the locket had been there and to whom it had belonged. Why was it here? Who would leave such a beautiful necklace behind? Mae dropped the locket carefully in her pocket, making a mental note to ask Cassie about the initials.

7

BITTERSWEET

Lucy, 1958

Lucy worked all summer long to restore the garden to its long-lost splendor. The barrage of floating butterflies, fuzzy bees bouncing from bloom to bloom, and sweetly chirping birds hopping between shrubs thanked her daily. She tenderly cut back the excessive growth and dead-headed the blooms that needed it in the fall to support their dormancy. The following spring when tiny green buds began to appear and life sprung up on every surface of the garden, Lucy couldn't help but feel a part of her own heart that had lay dormant after her father's passing also begin to sprout to life again.

Lying on the garden floor, Lucy closed her eyes and listened to the buzz of the natural world around her. Another year had passed since John's untimely accident, but Lucy was finally finding her footing again. She loved working at the newspaper and dared to dream of becoming a journalist there one day. Things at home, though still financially tight, seemed to be going well. Lucy continued to care for her siblings before and after work while her mother was cleaning houses, and while they had never returned to their previous level of closeness, the grief between Lucy and her mother healed enough that they could occasionally share a close moment, stolen between the shared responsibilities of running the household absent of a father. Time spent in this garden reminded Lucy of the cyclical nature of life. All things must be born, grow, thrive, and eventually die. While she understood the role and value of death in a garden, she wasn't quite sure how it worked with people. She had accepted it was a mystery of life that would never be revealed to her, just as thousands of people before her had accepted while descending the mountain of grief. For this moment now, sun warming her skin, Lucy felt hopeful.

"Whatcha doin' down there?" came the voice of Lucy's best friend, Patty.

Lucy smiled, knowing full well that Patty knew what she was doing, she just never understood why Lucy needed to lie in the dirt to feel peace. Patty sat on the ground next to Lucy, plucking a rogue blade of grass from the vegetable patch next to her and fidgeting with it between her fingers.

"What's going on, Patty? You seem nervous," Lucy assessed, pushing herself up to her elbows to meet Patty's gaze. Patty didn't make eye contact and instead focused on the blade of grass, twirling it between fingers.

Patty and Lucy had been inseparable friends since they both could remember. The first time they met, Patty and her mother brought a basket of homemade banana nut muffins over to introduce themselves to their new neighbors, having just moved in. Patty and Lucy were the same age, four at the time, and while at that first meeting, they hid behind their respective mother's legs out of shyness, a friendship grew after that day. They spent the long winters sledding, building snowmen, making snow angels, and the pair's favorite: snow forts. At the end of the driveway where the snowplow pushed the street snow over and around the mailbox was the perfect block for creating a fort. Patty and Lucy spent hours on their bellies digging their mittened hands through the dense snow, carving out a hollow space just big enough for the two to fit inside. They retreated indoors only once their hands were numb and clothes soaked through, thawing out by wrapping their tiny hands around warm mugs of cocoa and sitting by the wood-burning stove in Lucy's kitchen.

Come spring, Lucy and Patty liked to ride their bikes around neighborhoods and through the countryside, always stopping at a stream to perilously balance on slick rocks while hopping across, looking for unique rocks and drinking from the stream's clear water. They often had picnics in the woods, sitting under the shade of the trees with snacks packed in their backpacks. Once school was dismissed for the summer, the girls spent every day together, exploring in the critters of the backyard, finger painting while sprawled out on the kitchen floor, giggling over made-up storylines with their dolls. The girls' mothers loved that they had a confidant in each other and welcomed each girl in as their own when they didn't want to separate for dinner or even sleep, allowing them "camp-in" nights on each other's bedroom floors.

Lucy loved Patty like a sister, and Patty loved Lucy the same. After Lucy's dad died, Patty was there, checking in on Lucy daily, holding her while she cried, and stroking her hair as she fell into grief-stricken, exhaustion-fueled naps. Patty helped the family organize the funeral, made the family meals when they were too sorrowfully aloof to return to routine, and even acted as the family's proxy to nosey neighbors feigning concern while looking for gossip. Lucy knew Patty inside and out and could sense her emotions from proximity alone. On this day, while Patty sat next to her in the garden, wrapping a blade of grass around her delicate fingers, Lucy knew she had something to say that she was not going to like.

"Patty…" Lucy prodded, "out with it."

"Earl," Patty started, then paused. She focused her eyes to a point in the distance and inhaled a deep breath, then slowly sighed it out, steadying her voice. "Earl asked me to marry him." Patty held out her left hand, a beautifully modest engagement ring adorned her ring finger.

"Patty, that's great news! Congratulations," Lucy sat, taking Patty's sparkly hand in her own, trying to gauge why this news felt so solemn coming from Patty now.

Patty tried her hardest to keep her face neutral but was so sensitive to her friend's feelings that her mouth turned down and a tear eked out the corner of her eye. Lucy put her arm around her friend and pulled her into an embrace, still unsure of what to say.

"Hey, hey, what's going on here? Do you not want to? You love Earl. I love Earl. Everybody loves Earl," Lucy offered.

Patty wiped her eyes with the back of her hand and drew in another deep breath. "No, I know. I do. I love him and I do want to marry him. It's just that…" she hesitated. "He's done with basic training now and is being stationed at a base in Virginia."

"Virginia?" Lucy repeated, mouth slightly ajar in surprise.

"Next week," Patty finished.

"Next week?! But–" but Lucy had no other words. She felt like an anvil had just landed in the pit of her stomach.

Lucy was honest when she said she loved Earl. The inseparable friends had started dating another set of inseparable friends, Earl and Kurt, within weeks of each other. The foursome had spent countless hours together strolling the downtown streets, eating ice cream, and going to drive-in movies. Patty fell head-over-heels for Earl after their first date, and while Lucy had less passionate feelings for Kurt, he was a fine enough boyfriend for the dynamic of the group she wanted to maintain.

Earl decided to join the Air Force immediately after they finished high school, following in his own father's footsteps. Patty and Lucy were proud of the way he wanted to serve his country and provide for not only her but their future family, but somehow Lucy had never considered that his commitment to the military and to her friend would eventually mean taking Patty to a base far away. A heart full of conflicted emotions filled Lucy now with a swirling wave of love, heartbreak, pride, and sorrow all at once. Of course, she was happy for Patty and knew Patty wanted nothing more than to marry Earl and start a family with him. But selfishly, she wasn't ready for life to change so significantly again, after having to adjust to the death of one relationship already.

    Lucy spent the next week with Patty, preparing for her cross-country move, packing her belongings carefully into boxes as they dared to dream of what the future would hold for Patty and Earl. She helped her friend find a beautiful white lace dress at Margaret's Dress Shop in town and sat with her at the salon the day of her wedding, beaming at her beautiful friend becoming even more beautiful for her wedding day. Lucy and Kurt witnessed their friends' marriage with damp eyes and bittersweet love in their hearts from a cold courthouse bench, just six days after their garden conversation. The following day, Patty and Earl set out as a married couple to their new future, a thousand miles away.

    After seeing them off, Lucy made an excuse to Kurt so that she could be alone and retreated to her garden, again lying down, letting the ground support her. This time instead of hope, her heart filled with sadness that weighed her down like a bag of sand in her stomach. She let her tears flow and soak into the earth below her, wishing more than anything for those she loved most to stop leaving her.

8

STILL HERE

Mae, 2022

Mae settled into a routine over the next few weeks: morning walks or runs by the lake and breakfast at Cove Coffee, followed by working in the garden. A couple times a week she'd have dinner at The Crooked Cask's bar, taking in the locals' conversation and dice games and growing her friendship with Cassie. She felt more a member of the Cale Cove community with every passing day and grew fond of the town's unique residents. As her skin tanned and her palms calloused, Mae's pride in the garden grew. It was finally taking shape into what it might have once been.

Entering the garden today, Mae's eyes were drawn to the entrance stanchion, again spotting something sitting atop it. She was confused to discover it was what appeared to be a half-eaten sugar cookie littered with a kaleidoscope of multicolored sprinkles. Mae laughed to herself and looked around, not expecting, but still hoping, to discover which critter was leaving her these little gifts. Unsurprisingly, the yard was empty. Over the past few weeks, Mae had completely rid the garden of weeds, overgrown vines, and baby weed trees that had taken root, revealing not only the cement bench, but also carving out a space for neatly planted vegetable rows, surrounded by what she hoped were budding perennial flowers enveloping the space. The patch had been so unruly she hadn't before noticed the flowers, but now that the space was clear and the blooms had room to stretch toward the sky, she saw that the plants were everywhere. Mae didn't yet know the name of many things, but nonetheless appreciated the beauty of the ever-changing garden.

She had one row of virgin tilled soil remaining upon which she planned to plant more vegetables. She carried with her on this day a pocketful of seed packets and a wagon full of small vegetable plants she picked up from the local nursery on the outskirts of town. They had helped her select the varieties of tomatoes, squashes, beans, and cucumbers that would be most likely to succeed in her garden as well as be pleasing to her taste buds once it was time to harvest. The experts advised starting her vegetable garden from plants that were already several inches tall, but Mae wanted to try out seeds too, so she bought both.

As she sat in the dirt and placed the seed packets on the ground next to her, Mae thought of her interaction with Miles that morning, the warmth of which brought a smile to her face. Miles was amused by Mae's recent interest in rehabbing the neglected garden, and she discovered his penchant for horribly cheesy puns. She replayed the conversation in her head with flushed-face fondness.

"Well, if it isn't Cale Cove's master gardener in training," he said as Mae entered the cafe, the door's dangling bell announcing her arrival.

Mae laughed, replying, "I'm the master of one thing and that is a yard of chaos."

Miles paused for a moment, then raising an eyebrow teased, "So you're saying there's mushroom for improvement?"

"Let's just say it's a good thing I'm enjoying it because if it were a job, I'd be complaining about the low…celery."

"Oh, come on…" Miles laughed. "I'm sure it will be chicken proof by the time you're done."

Mae looked at him quizzically.

"Impeccable."

Mae exaggeratedly rolled her eyes. "OK, that was groan-worthy, Miles."

"OK, OK, well at least you're making friends in the garden. You know, so many buds." The two laughed at each other and held eye contact, enjoying the banter. Miles took Mae's order and let her enjoy her breakfast alone, but just as she was leaving, caught her at the door and said, "Hey Mae. Little gnome fact…I like working with my hands so if you need any help, gimme a holler."

She giggled again now recounting it, while considering taking him up on the offer. Mae worked the dirt in the remaining unplanted area, mixing in fertilizer from the nursery to ensure the ideal growing environment for her new plants. Working all afternoon, she planted the pre-started vegetables, pushed the seeds in the soil, and pulled the already reviving weeds in the other vegetable rows. As she finished up, her body felt tired and she rested on the ground, breathing heavily. Who knew gardening was actually hard physical work?

Mae laid down on her back, gazing up at the pale blue sky and the birds above flitting between trees, chirping happily. Puffy white clouds drifted lazily across the summer sky and the scent of freshly mowed lawns lingered in the air. Mae gently closed her eyes, drinking in the warmth of the sun on her cheeks. She wasn't sure why, but she had been carrying the locket in her pocket each day since she found it. Mae reached into her pocket and clasped her fingers around the mysterious necklace now, thinking of Grandma Lucy.

Today was the third anniversary of her passing and she missed her more than ever. Lucy would have loved this garden, and working in it somehow made Mae feel closer to her. Lucy would have known all of the names of the plants and exactly how to care for them. She'd be able to recognize any sign of sickness just by looking and would administer a remedy sure to heal. She would also know the names of all the weeds and even find joy in removing them, no matter how stubborn or spiny. "The only difference between a flower and a weed is a judgement. Nevertheless, we don't want them here," she could almost hear Lucy saying. Lucy was synonymous with gardening.

Mae's heavy eyes stayed closed, her exhausted body resting heavily on the soil as her breath slowed. She wondered what Lucy would think of the garden and all of the work she had put into it. She hoped she would be proud of Mae. What she would give for just one more conversation with her. Mae muttered to herself out loud, "I miss you Luce. I love you so much. I miss your company."

"I didn't go anywhere, honeybee, I've been here with you all along."

Mae's eyes snapped open, and she sat bolt upright upon hearing her grandmother's voice. Surely that was not just in her mind. Mae whipped her head around, heart thumping in her chest. Across the garden, sitting on the cement bench as if she had truly been there all along, was Mae's grandmother Lucy. Hands folded neatly in her lap, legs crossed at the ankle, and a genuine smile enveloping her entire face, it was unmistakably Lucy. Mae gaped, mouth ajar, questioning her own sanity and contemplating if she might be having a heatstroke or some kind of psychotic break. She looked around the yard, shuttered her eyes closed and open again, and looked back toward the bench. Lucy was still there.

Lucy laughed, her wide smile crinkling her eyes closed, her parted lips revealing the tiny gap in her front teeth that Mae loved. Her dark hair was streaked with gray and styled in the same wavy bob Mae remembered. She wore one of her bird shirts, as Mae called them, the kind only endearing old ladies wear with cardinals embroidered across the chest. Her soft, sun-spotted hands sat resting in her lap like she was patiently waiting for something. Mae rose from the ground, dirt clinging to the backs of her sweaty legs, while she made her way incredulously to the bench.

"Lucy, I…" Mae struggled to find words. "I can't believe this. What's happening? Is this a very, *very* realistic dream?"

"Isn't life just a dream?" Lucy replied airily, looking out across the garden. She patted the bench beside her. "Join me here."

Mae reached the bench and held out her arms to embrace her grandmother, but Lucy's face dropped for a moment. "We can't touch, honey. My body died in the physical sense, so we can't touch."

"But you're here…" Mae said, dropping her arms, eyes slowly filling with tears, still bewildered at her favorite person in the world sitting in front of her, in the flesh, but not? It wasn't like a ghost or apparition she'd seen on TV; Lucy wasn't translucent. There were no heavenly sparkles, and she wasn't backlit in an angelic ambience. It was just regular Lucy. Mae sat next to her on the bench, strangely feeling no warmth or presence as she would while sitting next to another body in any other context.

"I've always been here. Every day since my body died. I've never left you, Mae."

"I don't understand…"

"It's ok, baby, you don't need to. I just need you to know I never left, nor can I ever leave. I love you and you me and that links our souls across death. It only makes sense once you're on the other side of it," Lucy tried to explain.

"Other side of it…" Mae repeated. "It? Life?"

Lucy nodded.

"But…how can I see you? How is this possible?" Mae's mind raced with so many questions for which not even the religious, dogmatic upbringing she experienced could possibly explain. I've missed you for so long and now you're here and I can't even come up with what to say. It's just," Mae could barely put a sentence together, "so good to see you." She blinked, letting a hot tear fall from each eye, streaking its path through the dirt and sweat on her cheeks. It wasn't sadness she felt, but an overwhelming wave of love only experienced upon seeing someone you've missed so much it physically hurt.

Lucy held Mae's gaze with so much love in her eyes, then tilted her head back as she laughed again. "I'd say the same, but I've been seeing you all along! And it's always a pleasure. Beautiful as ever, my little Mae, taking the world by storm."

"I don't know about that, grandma." Mae's shoulders slumped as she looked down at her lap, studying her dirt-encrusted fingernails. "This year has been a bit of a shit show, if you don't mind my language," Mae said. Lucy never minded vulgarity and reveled in real talk. She valued genuine emotion, not the mask many people put on in front of others while obscuring their true emotions. "There's so much to tell you about with my job and…"

"I know about your job and the boy. And, oh honey, I know it feels some type of way right now, but sometimes a lesson looks a lot like bullshit," Lucy offered. "Sometimes you need to get a little lost and a little thrown off course to realize the course wasn't ever what you thought it was going to be." A moment passed and Lucy added, "For what it's worth, I think you've handled it marvelously. Look at this patch of beauty you've resurrected," Lucy gestured to the garden surrounding them.

Mae gazed out, surveying the space she'd poured so much into. She felt a touch of pride well up inside her and was grateful for her grandmother's perspective, presence, and just to hear her voice again. Across the yard was a family of sandhill cranes, approaching cautiously. One met her eye and delicately stretched its neck over the stone fence wall to pluck a mulberry off of a tree. Mae watched it, and it watched her back.

"The strangest things have been happening with animals around here, Luce. Do you ever feel like they're watching you?" Mae said, looking over at Lucy again, but Lucy was no longer there. Just as quickly as she came to mysteriously occupy the bench, the seat was now vacant. "Lucy?!" Mae spun around, frantically looking for her grandmother, to no avail. Mae stood and walked around the garden, hoping a different vantage point would somehow disprove what she already knew. Lucy was simply gone.

    Mae sat back down on the bench, feeling the full weight of her exhaustion. Surely, she was losing her mind. How was it even possible? Maybe she drifted off when she was lying in the dirt, but she was definitely awake now. Mae pinched her arm hard, feeling a sharp pain. Yes, she was definitely awake now. But Lucy was here! She heard her, she saw her. What was happening? She gripped the locket in her pocket and ran her fingertips over the etching in the metal, enraptured by what had unfolded. Mae sat there for several minutes, replaying what just happened in her head. Eventually, resigned to the mystery, she decided to go inside and leave the garden behind for the day.

9

NEVER LEFT

Lucy, 1958

In the several weeks after Patty left town, Lucy couldn't bring herself to work in the garden. Her sadness sunk deep into her bones such that the only activities for which she could muster the energy to do were work, caretaking for her siblings, and the occasional date with Kurt. She missed the days when life felt easy. Being carefree and playing with Patty, fishing with her dad, reading endless novels by the fire at night. When did the weight of responsibility get so heavy? It rained in Cale Cove for ten straight days, the atmosphere mimicking the emotions locked away in Lucy.

    On an overcast but dry weekend morning, Lucy gazed out her second-story bedroom window at the garden she had not stepped foot in for weeks. The heaviness of losing Patty kept her away from it, but seeing the weeds take over and the dead blooms that needed pruning made her heart ache in such a way that she knew she had to get back to tending it. Lucy's eye caught a deer walking through the yard, stopping just short of the garden. As Lucy watched it, the deer pointedly looked at the garden, surveying the space, then unmistakably looked straight at Lucy through the window. Lucy looked around, but knew full well it was her the deer was looking at because she was in the house, alone in the bedroom, and what else would it be looking at up here? They continued to lock eyes while the deer blinked and continued to watch Lucy. Lucy's gaze swept the yard and returned to the deer, still watching unflinchingly from its post. Fine, you win, thought Lucy.

She changed clothes and headed out to the garden, the deer watching her all the while. Its persistence made Lucy grin as she got down on her knees and started pulling the relentless weeds. She worked for hours returning the once-stunning patch of earth to its former beauty, pruning, pulling, shaping, and raking until her fingers ached, her low back tightened from bending over, and a cool layer of sweat covered her brow. Lucy wrapped her fingers around the last offending weed, a giant thistle, gripping it tightly and pulling it from the base. When it didn't budge, she wrapped her other hand around it, now pulling it full force with both hands on the weed, her feet planted on the ground. She gave it a firmer yank and it broke off, sending the force of her stumbling back and falling over.

Lucy stayed splayed out on the ground laughing, feeling the joy of communing with nature coming back to her. She reflected on the cycles of the garden, thankful that the dire state of it was never final. Always growing and changing, adapting to its environment and care, perhaps her heart could be the same. Perhaps she could make it out from under the pressing weight of sadness that had taken up residence in her chest, a perpetual pressure that never seemed to relent. The garden was resurrected and looked colorful and vibrant as ever. The morning clouds had lifted, and the sun was peeking out from behind them now, warming Lucy's face as she gazed up toward it. Exhausted, Lucy allowed her eyes to get heavy and close for a moment.

She dreamt of her dad joining her in this backyard respite he had maintained all the years of her life until he had passed. In the dream, her dad took a break from planting, sitting on the cement bench at the edge of the garden. He peeled off his sweaty, dirt-covered gloves and tossed them on the ground, wiping his palms on his blue jeans. Lucy sat next to him, and they shared a comfortable silence, as if he had never died and this was something they did together often.

Relishing in the closeness of her dad, Lucy broke the silence, "I've missed you, dad. I wish we could have done this together," referring to gardening. When John was alive, Lucy showed little interest in the garden, but maintaining it now was her only physical connection to him.

"We do, kiddo. I'm here all the time," John replied.

Lucy's heart was heavy in his presence, weighed down by all of the might-have-beens and should-bes. The years she expected them to have together that would never happen. All the fish they didn't get to catch together. The graduation stage he'd never see her walk. The wedding aisle he didn't get to walk her down. The grandchildren he never got to meet or hold. The child-rearing and life advice she didn't even know she needed yet but that would never be dispensed. And all of the embraces she took for granted but would never again feel. The lucidity of the dream didn't prevent Lucy from knowing that her dad was in fact dead. Gone. Never to be hugged again.

"I've missed you," she said again, throat swelling with the bittersweetness of their meeting. "I love you so much, dad."

John turned to Lucy, his own deep brown eyes glassy, and a warm smile deepened the creases in his cheeks, its edges spanning his face like an all-embracing sunset. "I love you too, kid. I'm really proud of what you've done here."

Lucy let her tears fall. As they escaped her eyelashes and dropped onto her lap, they were filled with more than sorrow. They were the release of the overflowing love in her heart, spilling out her eyes. "I just don't understand why you had to go. It wasn't your time yet. We still need you."

"I know it hurts, Luce, but death must come for all things. Everything is cyclical. Even this garden. You've seen this through the changing of seasons and what beauty death brings forth for the earth." John paused to let his words sink in, then continued, "Death is not an error or a failure, kiddo. It's part of life."

"But I love you," Lucy said, half hoping that love could root his physical presence in reality again.

"And I you, kid. And that's why we'll keep loving each other. I don't need to be in a physical body for us to do that. Every time you think of me and act in a way that I taught you or inspired you to do, you're keeping me alive. I am alive, just in a different way. I'm always with you." Lucy's chest swelled with the warmth of having a conversation with her dad again. Unable to fully grasp his wisdom, she accepted his words in silence, trying to imprint every word into her memory to turn over in her mind later.

"Hey, listen. I never got to give you your birthday present," John reached into his pocket, cupping something in his hand. "Close your eyes and hold out your hands."

Lucy loved this game. They used to play it all the time when she was young, delivering each other little treats, unique rocks, feathers, or even worms when they fished together. Lucy turned eighteen after her dad's accident, but now learned her father had already planned a gift for her. Knowing this made her heart swell with appreciation. She stuck her hands out in front of her, palms face up, excitedly anticipating what the delivery would be this time.

John placed a cool, metal object in her hands and said, "OK, open them!" In her hands sat a beautiful, heart-shaped, white-gold locket. She turned it over to discover her initials, *LAM,* engraved on it. She gasped sharply, stunned by the gift.

"Dad...it's beautiful! I love it so much," she exclaimed.

"Here, I'll put it on you," John offered. Lucy handed him the necklace and pulled her hair off of her neck to allow him to clasp it. The locket sat delicately on her chest, and she marveled at it, holding it close to her.

"Open it up," John directed.

Lucy pried open the locket and found two pictures inside. One showed John kneeling next to a little Lucy, the two of them with one arm around each other's shoulders, the other arm holding a fish each, radiant smiles pouring from each of their faces. The other photo was of Lucy's biggest catch—a fifteen-inch walleye. John beamed with pride that day at Lucy's catch and she felt like a master fisherman when they brought the fish home and grilled it for dinner that night.

"Dad, thank you. This is so wonderful."

"I'm glad you like it. It was supposed to be for your 18th, but now it can be your reminder that I'm always with you." Lucy beamed at her dad and felt her grief-stricken longing retreat. She shared this moment with her dad, looking into his chocolate brown eyes as he grinned and diverted his eyes to his lap, always a little uncomfortable with intimate moments.

A fat raindrop fell on Lucy's face, rolling into her eye, promptly awakening her from her backyard catnap. She remained lying on the garden floor as her eyes batted open, taking in her surroundings. It was a dream, of course. The sadness returned as she remembered that her dad really was dead, and she couldn't have just spoken with him. The rain fell harder as each moment passed, so Lucy gathered herself up off the ground, starting for the house. Her head was swirling with all that she'd seen and felt in the dream. Was it a dream? It had felt so real, like her dad wasn't gone anymore. Like he had somehow just gone away for a couple years, and it was all a strange diversion of what life should be.

A loud crack of thunder and sky-splitting lightning illuminated the cloud-covered sky as Lucy ran faster up the yard. As she entered the house, she closed the door behind her and paused, leaning against it for several moments. The rain pattered on the pane as her pulse throbbed in her temples. She closed her eyes and took a deep breath, her hand finding its way to her neck, where her fingers settled around a white gold, heart-shaped locket.

10

LOST CONNECTION

Mae, 2022

Mae had spent so much time in the garden that it had been over a week since her last run. As she stepped down the path toward the lake, she deepened her breathing, settling into a comfortable pace. The familiar internal voice of critique returned to Mae's mind.

"Well, isn't it nice of you to be running midday without a care in the world, without a job either."

While Mae loved getting to know her new town and work in a garden that wasn't actually hers over the past few weeks, the annoyingly practical part of her worried she was treating this as a vacation and needed to snap back to the reality of finding a job soon.

Her internal voice relentlessly continued, "Did you really think you could just waltz into a new life in a new town and forget that you were a big, fat failure at your last job? Good luck finding a new one and explaining how you were FIRED."

How was she supposed to find a new job if the one thing she thought she was good at, the world had proven to her otherwise? Her confidence was shaken. And then there was Jared. Was she too hard on him after all? Sure, they disagreed about the fundamental future of their relationship, but they had fun times together. There was something there that attracted her initially; did she throw that away too quickly? No relationship was perfect, after all. Maybe her mother was right, and she should have "hung onto" him.

The perpetual feed of engagement and pregnancy announcements that flooded her social media feeds daily only sharpened the sting of the suspicion Mae just wasn't where she should be by now. Mae picked up the pace as she neared the lake, appreciating the view but not wanting to linger today. There was an energy in her body, in her legs, that she needed to unleash.

Mae hated it when she got into her own head like this, yet she couldn't seem to stop it. Who did she think she was convincing everyone in Cale Cove that she was this happy-go-lucky out-of-towner who just happened to be the perfect addition to their town?

"This kind of thing only happens in Nicholas Sparks books, and you, Mae Montgomery, are not in a Nicholas Sparks book," she reminded herself.

Soon enough they'd know she was only here out of a desperate need to escape her old life, the corporate world having laughed her out of the big city, ejecting her into this small town with her dignity barely intact. Yep, she'd be found out soon. They would all know the hot mess express she was, and she wouldn't be fooling them much longer.

Mae slowed to a walk as she returned to her rented home and headed to the backyard for a survey of the newly-improved garden. She had finished all of the major work she intended to do with the garden and was now sitting on the bench, assessing it from a distant perspective, deciding what to do next. She could divide the bordering hostas and distribute them around more of the perimeter of the garden, though if she did that, she should probably clean the mildew off the fence. Maybe a nice trellis with a grape vine? That would be dreamy.

As Mae tried to contemplate garden plans, her mind diverted back to making sense of her encounter with Lucy. It made no logical sense that she had a conversation with her dead grandmother in this garden, but she also couldn't tear her thoughts from it since it happened. She hadn't told anyone about it, not even Cassie, despite their vast conversations. Mae knew logically it was improbable and yes, she had a creative mind, but she was sure that she could not have made it up. Perhaps she wanted to hold on to the possibility that she could still talk to and hang out with Lucy, but she wasn't ready to give up that hope just yet.

Mae walked through the garden, up and down the vegetable rows taking stock of things. Nothing needed weeding or pruning today, which allowed her to meander aimlessly. She returned to the bench, allowing the cool cement to soothe her wandering mind, eyes unfocused across the yard, allowing her thoughts to drift. Several moments passed, then suddenly she was startled by a voice beside her.

"You know what would be great here is a koi pond." Mae's eyes shot back into focus, head spinning to the bench beside her, where Lucy sat again.

"LUCY!" Mae yelled.

Mae knew she couldn't hug her, but her arms flung wide as if she could. "I knew it was real! I knew I didn't make this up!"

Lucy chuckled, "Of course it's real, honey. Why the hell wouldn't it be?"

"I don't know, it's just...well. Lucy, you're dead. And yet, you're here. It's not like any of this really makes any sense."

"Death is neither here nor there," Lucy replied with a casual wave of her hand, "it's all just an illusion really."

Mae's mind was reeling, her words jumbled before she could speak them aloud, rendering her mute. She opened her mouth a few times as if to speak, but promptly closed it when she realized she had no idea what to say. This was all so incredibly ridiculous. And she didn't care one bit.

"A koi pond sounds marvelous," Mae finally said, grinning at Lucy.

"Mae…*you who*," a woman's sing-song voice carried through the yard, catching Mae's attention.

"I'm back here!" Mae called. She glanced back at Lucy, but the empty bench beside her confirmed her suspicion that Lucy had left. Knowing this time that it was only temporary, Mae wasn't sad. She recognized Patty's form making its way through the yard to the garden, holding a small tray in her hands, a dog bounding in front of her.

"I brought you some treats, honey! Care for some iced tea and cookies?" Patty asked.

"Those are two things I will never say no to! C'mon let's go up to the porch where there's a table," Mae suggested. Then she offered, "Let me help you with that." Mae seized the tray from Patty and Patty gratefully accepted, being a little unsteady on her feet on the knobby lawn.

As they walked up the yard and toward the porch, the friendly dog kept pace with them. Mae said, "This must be Buster."

"Oh yes, he's very friendly. He's an old guy now but still likes to bounce around. Miles should be by shortly to take him for his daily walk. Bless that man's heart, he does that for me every day," Patty explained.

They settled in on the porch, each reclining in a chair, Buster plopping down between them. Mae sipped the tea and took a bite of cookie. She closed her eyes and marveled at the explosion of flavor in each. "Oh my god, Patty. These are incredible! Is this peppermint tea?"

"It is! Made with my own mint leaves grown out back. Of course, I added a bit of sugar to sweeten it up a bit," she said with a wink.

"And these cookies…how are they *so* lemony?!"

"The secret is both lemon juice *and* zest," Patty said, delighted at Mae's excitement.

Mae enjoyed the rest of her cookie in silence, reverence really. They were a true baking wonder. "Thank you so much for sharing them with me."

"It's my pleasure, honey! You've been working so hard out in that garden and running all over the place, we need to plump you back up. Need a grandma in your life to feed you cookies," Patty chuckled to herself, patting Mae affectionately on the knee. Mae could imagine she would be a lovely grandma. Warm and friendly, her house smelling of baked goods, and a soft dog to cuddle up with.

"Are your grandkids close?" Mae asked, assuming that Patty was indeed a grandma.

"Sadly, no. My older son, William, lives in New York with his partner and they don't have kids, and my younger son, Peter, is out in the San Francisco Bay Area with his three little ones. Oh, I do love them so, but they're only around here usually for a bit in the summer and the holidays."

"Well, if you're ever looking for a taste tester, I would gladly oblige," Mae offered with a mischievous grin.

"Noted," Patty laughed. "Now who's this strapping young man?!"

"Ah, Patty, you flatter me." Miles was walking up the sidewalk to the porch now, hands in his khaki chinos' pockets with his thumbs sticking out, dog leash draped around his shoulders. He was wearing his black Cove Coffee polo shirt, having interrupted his workday to come here. His long stride delivered him from the sidewalk to the porch in just a few steps, where he casually leaned on the porch railing, crossing one foot in front of the other. Mae felt her pulse quicken.

"Hey Miles."

"Well, hello there. I've come to relieve you of this little mutt," Miles said, dropping to his knees to envelope Buster's face in his hands. He tussled the dog's ears as it licked his face. He hooked the leash around Buster's collar and stood again.

"Now I know you're not trying to get out of here without a cookie or two," Patty insisted, pushing herself from her chair to offer the tray to Miles.

Miles patted his stomach with a laugh, "Does it look like I've ever denied you from feeding me, Patty? Will you two be here when I get back?"

Patty looked at Mae, eyebrows raised in question.

Mae tried to quell her nerves with another sip of tea, "I'm here all day," she finished with a nervous laugh she tried to make casual.

"Alright, I'll see you ladies in a bit," Miles replied with a tip of his imaginary hat. He and Buster set off down the sidewalk toward downtown.

Patty smirked at Mae, putting the tray back on the table. She looked back at Miles walking away, then back at Mae with an even bigger grin on her face.

"Patty no," Mae said.

"I said nothing," Patty shrugged, miming a zipper closing her mouth.

Mae laughed, "If he was interested, he would have said something by now." While she listened to the words leave her mouth, she hoped they weren't true. She was curious about Miles; she had been since the first day she walked into Cove Coffee. Then she had cut herself off from being interested because she knew she needed to heal from Jared, but she felt all of the alone time she'd spent in the garden had mended her heart. While she still did feel a little bit like a failure, she was sure that particular relationship was a success she didn't want and that she made the right move to leave him in the past.

Mae turned back to Patty, "I have to admit you're the last person I thought might be a wing woman for me. But honestly, you remind me a lot of my grandma, Lucy. Mischievous, a great baker, warm and loving…"

"Yeah," Patty paused, wistfully recalling memories, "Lucy was a wonderful woman, wasn't she?"

"Wait...what?" Mae was confused.

Patty hesitated, "I uh...I knew your grandma, honey."

"Lucy? My Lucy? Grandma Lucy. Lucinda Brown...er, Monroe then, I guess?"

"That's the one." Patty knew Lucy? How? And why would Patty be reluctant about this hidden fact?

"No way! Patty, that's amazing! What a crazy, small world," Mae exclaimed.

"It is indeed," Patty replied, no longer smiling.

"Why does it look like you wish you hadn't known her?" Mae inquired.

Patty paused, letting a moment of silence sit between them, heavy in the thick humidity of the day. "That's not it at all. Lucy was a really good friend of mine, the best friend. We were inseparable from the day we met each other at just four years old. But you know, life happened, and we drifted apart. It's one of my biggest regrets."

"I'm so sorry." Mae paused, then asked, "How did that happen?"

"I'm sure you know, Lucy's daddy died young. We couldn't have been more than seventeen at the time, and it was hard on their family. Lucy was the oldest. I think her mother expected a lot from her after his passing. Lucy went from a girl to a caregiver for her younger siblings overnight when her mother had to return to work herself. Lucy finished up high school alright, but I know she had her heart set on college. Girls didn't go to college much back then, especially not from a small town like Cale Cove, but..."

"Wait, Lucy was born here?" Mae interrupted.

"Of course, honey, that's how I knew her," Patty looked surprised that Mae didn't know this.

"All this time I thought she was born in Illinois, where she'd always been. I think we all thought so anyway..." Mae trailed off. "Sorry, continue."

Patty nodded and continued, "So girls back then didn't go to college much, not like they do now, but I know Lucy wanted to study creative writing and be the next Jane Austen. And she could have! That girl's pen knew no bounds. She was an incredible storyteller, weaving beautifully intricate storylines and characters with such depth you wouldn't believe! I loved reading anything she wrote. But Lucy knew that with her father gone, her mother didn't have the money to send her to college and sure as heck couldn't afford to lose Lucy's help around the house.

"So, Lucy secured a job as a secretary at the newspaper in town and settled in there. I think she thought working her way to a reporting job might be a compromise to her creative writing dream. We dated friends back then—I was with Earl and Lucy was with Kurt. We four got up to a lot together in the summertime, going to drive-in movies together and weekend ice creams at Wally's. Swimming at the lake. We were inseparable. I think when I got engaged was the beginning of the end of Lucy and me."

"Such a happy thing though," Mae lamented.

"It was. Lucy was a great friend and she loved Earl and knew how much I loved Earl, but it was quick, I know. Earl had joined the Air Force and while we had talked about marriage before he had to leave for his duties, I didn't bother Lucy with that burden. She had enough going on in her heart and head at the time. But if I would have, maybe it wouldn't have been such a shock when I told her we were getting married in a week and moving away."

"Oh. Wow."

"I know. It was a lot. Lucy was the best friend as ever though, helping me with the arrangements and 'oohing' and 'aahing' over every dress I tried on at Margaret's," Patty remembered with a laugh, then continued, "And we did. We got married a week later and set out across the country on our new life, Earl as an airman and me as a military wife. Little did I know I had William already in my belly then."

Patty's hand moved unconsciously to her lower stomach, remembering.

"We stayed in touch writing letters often, but as soon as William came, well, life changed very quickly. I was busy and tired and lonely all at the same time, but I felt like I either couldn't convey that over a letter, or I shouldn't. Lucy had been through so much that what did she care that I chose to marry a man who wouldn't be around very much while I had a little baby at home? That was life then, everybody did it, so why should I complain about it? Anyway, we did stay in touch for a while, but when Lucy married, moved, and had her own brood, the letters eventually stopped. Raising kids is a full-time job, and we were both doing it with little help, in a town where we knew no one. I always wished that we'd reconnected later in life, but we never did."

"Gosh, Patty," Mae sat contemplating, "I'm so sorry."

"I am, too, honey. I am, too," Patty lamented. The pair sat in silence, tray of cookies between them on the porch, both lost in thought of their apparent linked past.

Mae broke the silence. "Wait, how did you know I'm Lucy's granddaughter?"

The sound of a male voice interrupted Patty's thoughts, "Now that this fella has terrorized every squirrel in Cale Cove, I return him to you." Miles stepped back up to the porch, tying Buster's leash loosely on the porch railing and taking a seat beside him on the floor, crossing his legs like a child at a campfire.

Mae could be mistaken, but Patty's warm face flickered with a sense of relief with the return of Miles and Buster. She quickly forgot their previous conversation and instead said, "Welcome back you two! Can I offer you some cookies now?" Patty reached for the tray, but Miles motioned for her to stay seated while he stretched and grabbed a cookie from the flowered metal serving tray.

A bit of cookie already in his mouth, Miles closed his eyes and moaned, "Patty, the lemon ones!"

"I knew you'd be excited about those," Patty said, satisfied.

"How do they keep getting better?" Miles mumbled through a full mouth. Mae laughed at him and handed him a napkin, to which Miles tipped his head in thank-you.

The three of them chatted together about the weather, Buster's affinity for terrorizing woodland creatures, and how things at the cafe were going. After several minutes, Patty stood, brushing her button-down linen dress flat, and collecting the serving tray.

"It's getting to be about time for my afternoon nap, so I'm going to leave you kids here," Patty said. They thanked her for the cookies and tea and watched her return to her house next door. After Patty's door squeaked closed, Mae was suddenly aware that she was alone with Miles on her porch, probably already acting awkward in his presence. Mae reflexively looked to her feet for a distraction, noticing there was a piece of peeled paint stuck to her toe. Reaching down to remove it, Miles laughed.

"This porch has been needing a facelift for a couple years now. I didn't get around to it before putting the place up for rent. Any chance you'd be OK with me stopping by to do that sometime this week?"

"Yeah, of course. It's your house. I'll be around if you need any help," Mae said casually.

"Not *technically* mine, but great! I would love the help, or even just the company. Rehabbing this house was largely a solo endeavor. That is, except for Patty's drop-ins. She sustained me on cookies and iced tea," Miles laughed nostalgically.

"She's a pretty great neighbor," Mae replied.

Miles stood, adjusted his pants that had hiked, and ran a hand through his tousled hair. "Thanks for the offer to help, Mae, see you, let's say…Saturday morning?"

"Perfect."

Miles left with a wave and walked off toward the coffee shop, and Mae remembered he'd probably be going back to work. Walking Buster was just a lunch break. Work, right. She needed to start thinking more about getting a job again before her severance ran out. She'd been careful about her spending and since being in Cale Cove, realized that living here was quite a bit cheaper than in Chicago, so she knew she could stretch three months into four, maybe longer, but didn't want to push it. Could she work in Cale Cove? Should she look for something remote? Start growing more vegetables, get some chickens and goats, live off the land and stick it to capitalism? Just then her phone buzzed. A text from Cassie.

"Miss you girl. Dinner tonight?"

Mae smiled and let her fingers tap out, "Yes please."

Mae met Cassie at the Crooked Cask just as the sun was dipping in the sky, threatening a beautiful sunset over the lake. The Crooked Cask's back patio had a perfect view of sunsets over the lake and was usually full of couples, families, and friends drinking, dining, and playing board games most summer evenings. Mae was surprised that despite working there, Cassie didn't mind hanging out at the Cask too. Sure, they could have gone elsewhere but Mae had fallen head-over-heels in love with the Cask's braised short rib-topped nachos.

Biting into a chip topped with the perfect balance of melted cheese, short rib, jalapeño, and sour cream, Mae said, "They are truly a gift from the heavens sent here by a higher power who clearly loves us and wants us to be happy." Mae closed her eyes while she finished chewing.

Cassie sat back in her chair and laughed, beer mug in hand, "I don't think I've seen anyone enjoy them as much as you, and I must say it's a true honor to witness," Cassie snorted, lifting her glass in a cheers.

Mae dabbed her mouth with a napkin and washed it all down with a sip of beer. She started to tell Cassie about the interaction she had with Patty on the porch earlier that day, "It was this weird small-town coincidence. How could she possibly know my grandma? And how did she know that I was her granddaughter? I mean, sure, we share some similarities but nothing that's so striking you'd just *know* from looking, you know? The whole thing is peculiar."

"What did she say when you asked her how she knew you're Lucy's granddaughter?" Cassie asked.

"She didn't! Miles interrupted to return Buster after taking him for a walk," Mae said sadly.

"Take Buster for a walk?"

"Yeah, he apparently isn't already a handsome and nice enough cafe owner serving the best coffee in town, he also walks old ladies' dogs during his lunch break," Mae said snarkily.

Cassie laughed and drank another sip from her mug. "That Miles, serving up all the small-town charm that can fit in one man."

After Mae finished her nachos, she cleaned her hands with a wet wipe from the table caddy and brought the locket out of her pocket, setting it on the table. "Hey Cass, I've been meaning to ask you about this. I found it in my backyard when I was digging around in the dirt, and I thought maybe you might know the initials since you know a lot about Cale Cove."

Cassie leaned forward and turned the locket over in her hand. She ran her fingers over the etched letters and quietly thought. "L-A-M," she said contemplatively, "I'm not sure, Mae. When I was a kid, the Robertsons lived in that house and before that I don't know. The historical society might have some info on the address. You could try there?"

"Yeah, maybe," Mae replied. "It's pretty, isn't it? I wonder how long it's been buried back there."

The two friends sat in silence for a few minutes, enjoying their drinks and the deepening pinks and oranges of the sunset. The din of neighboring tables faded around them as Mae's heart filled with a deep appreciation for this town that she'd found herself drawn to, the friendships she'd already made, and the beauty of the lake and sunsets she was privy to witness on a daily basis. Why would anyone ever want to leave Cale Cove?

11

BACK TO REALITY

Lucy, 1958

Since Lucy had discovered the ability to see and talk to her dad in the garden, she had visited him numerous times. They spent hours together talking, laughing, and enjoying each other's presence, as if he had never died. Lucy's heart felt whole again in a way she never imagined was possible after losing her father at such a formative age. John was able to tell her he was proud of her and listen to how she had adjusted to life in her new role at home and at the newspaper. Lucy had taken to not only visiting her dad after work but sometimes during her lunch break as well. When her mother was at work and her siblings were at school, she'd take the lunch she had packed herself in the morning and walk home, enjoying it in the garden with her dad's company, returning to work after and cleaning out her lunch box at the end of the day as if she had eaten at work.

Lucy wasn't sure why she kept the garden conversations from her mother but after a while of doing so, it seemed more and more a necessary secret to keep. It wasn't that she was selfish in wanting to keep her dad to herself; no, she would have loved it if her mother could talk to him, too. But the invisible divide that had forged itself between the Lucindas had grown deeper and more silent as time went on.

It forced cordiality instead of honesty, demure interactions instead of deep conversations. Lucy wasn't sure there was a way back, so she settled into the relative peace, if not disconnected loneliness, which had fallen over the Brown household in the absence of its head.

One particularly cloudy afternoon, Lucy had completed her typical after-work routine of prepping dinner and getting her younger siblings settled with a snack and their homework. She usually had a spare bit of time before she needed to start cooking and her mother returned home, so she meandered back to the garden to meet her dad. John was waiting there, a content grin spread across his face.

"How ya doin', kid?" he asked.

"Hey dad! I'm alright." Lucy joined her father on the cement bench and began catching her dad up on life lately. It had been a few days since she was able to make it out to the garden between a few big news days leading to late hours and getting their house ready to host an end-of-summer neighborhood get together. Lucy had big news to share and wasn't sure how her father would take it.

"Dad, I have something to tell you," Lucy started cautiously.

"What's goin' on?" John asked curiously.

"You remember Kurt…" Lucy waited for confirmation and at her father's nod continued with a deep breath, "we've been dating still, I guess, and I don't know if it's because Earl and Patty got married and moved but he uh…well he proposed to me. Last night."

John's eyebrows shot up in genuine surprise and stayed quiet for a moment. He studied his hands for the right words, but when nothing came, he rested on, "That's big news. How come I don't see a ring?"

"Because I didn't give him an answer," Lucy replied.

"Luce…you can't leave a guy hanging like that."

"I know. It's just…I don't know. I…" Lucy paused, looking for the right words for her emotion, but they simply didn't exist. She rolled many words around in her mouth and somehow settled on, "I don't know." Lucy's dad never gave his direct opinion on anyone she dated—he preferred that she make her own decisions and mistakes—and he wasn't about to start now.

"What's your hesitation?" he asked.

Lucy thought for a minute, nervously tucking her hair behind her ears. She tried to explain, "I thought it would feel different. That I would feel excited. The thought of marrying someone who's fine," she paused, steadying her hands and on her legs, smoothing the fabric under them, "just fine… without my dad there to walk me down the aisle and with things with mom as they are. I don't know, it's just all wrong. It's not how it's supposed to be."

"I know it's hard, Lucy. I didn't think it would be like this either. At a point though, honey, you've gotta release how you thought things were supposed to be and be here for what they are. I don't want you to punish yourself or withhold certain life experiences because I'm not there like you thought I'd be. I am here, always in your heart and never too far for a conversation," John said.

"I know, dad. I know. I'll get there." Lucy fixated on a blade of grass, willing the hot tears behind her eyes to stay where they were.

"Who are you talking to, Antoinette?!" Lucy's mother's sharp voice came from behind her. Lucy immediately flushed, heartbeat racing. She was no longer alone in the garden with her dad. Her mother was making her way across the lawn to join them. Only now Lucy focused her eyes on where her dad was, Lucy was sad to see he'd gone.

Lucy's mother was traipsing the lawn at a fast clip, catching up to her position quickly. Her skirt rustled the blades of grass in a brisk manner that matched her demeanor as she moved. "I finished work early," she managed to say through a look somewhere between confusion, fury, and indignance that Lucy couldn't quite read. "What are you doing out here? Who are you talking to?"

"Um…no one," Lucy said, attempting to sound casual and not at all like she was talking to her dead dad.

"Lucy, I saw you talking to somebody. Who else is here?" she asked with a glance sweeping side to side, coming up vacant. She stared at Lucy quizzically.

Lucy considered her two options: let her mom into her secret and hope she understood or keep lying her pants off and keep it to herself. The years since her father passed and her best friend had married and moved away left Lucy tired. She was weary from the grief, from the unmet expectations, from reconciling how she thought reality should be with how it turned out to be. She was tired of the distance with her mother and dancing around the subject of her dad as if mentioning him detonated a bomb in her mother's heart that could level everything around them. Lucy resigned to the moment, pressed her fingers to her temples, and sighed. "Sit down, mom."

Lucy's mother looked confused but obliged her daughter and joined her on the cement bench at the edge of the garden, the very place her late husband had occupied mere moments before. "I have to tell you something," Lucy said for the second time this afternoon. Her pulse quickened and she could feel her chest flush in nervous anticipation. Her fingers fidgeted with the hem on her shirt as she started, "I was talking to someone, mother. I was talking to dad." Her eyes avoided her mother's for several moments, then met them sidelong. Her mother seemed stoic.

"I don't know why you would say such a ridiculous thing to me, Antoinette. You and I both know he is gone," she said breathlessly.

"He is," Lucy replied, "but he's also not." The next words came out so quickly and in such a flurry she wasn't sure if her mother would catch all of them, "I started working in this garden—his garden—because I was sad and I don't know, maybe hoping that it would bring me closer to him somehow and it did! He shows up here, mama! He shows up here when I'm here and sits on this bench," she gestured with a finger, "and we talk. About my day, about life, about things before he was gone, everything. Everything and nothing and it's so wonderful. I don't understand it, but it's helped me feel less alone knowing that I can still see him and talk to him, and it could be really good for you, too." Lucy sucked in the deep breath she had been holding off for fear that if she stopped to breathe, she may not get all of her words about before her mother interjected. After her mother said nothing, she took another few deep breaths to calm her shaking hands.

"Have you lost your mind?" she said finally.

Lucy's chest sunk, deflating all of the hope she held of this strange occurrence being some sort of a bonding moment, a stepping stone over the unrelenting river of grief that stood between them. "Mama, if you just…"

"I don't need to 'just' anything. Nobody expected to lose your father when we did but we've all had to pick up and move on. I'm out of the house every day working, trying to fill the void that he left, trying to keep this house running as it should. You have the audacity to escape to the back yard and pick flowers while spinning some wild fantasy about how what I saw with my own eyes didn't actually happen."

"That's not what I said mama, it *did* happen of course, but…" Lucy tried to explain.

"Do *not* interrupt me, young lady," her mother scolded Lucy as if she was a petulant child misbehaving in a church pew. Her face grew redder with each word, a strand of hair escaping her neat bun as she spoke. "You cannot continue to live in this *fantasy* world of yours, Antoinette. The sooner you grow up and accept reality, the better it will be for us all. Can you imagine? Talking to your father out here all this time. You've got to be kidding me. He would be *so* disappointed in your aversion to moving on and your insistence on playing these childish games."

Lucy fought back tears. "He is not disappointed in me," she managed to say with tears burning behind her eyes.

"We raised you girls to become doting wives and mothers, as our parents did before us, and you're out here playing with dirt when there's a perfectly good man looking to make you the kind of homemaker you could only dream of." When Lucy's face turned from resigned to surprised, her mother continued, "Oh yes, I've talked to Kurt's mother already, to apologize for your hesitation in accepting the proposal of a very nice young man. Why must you make things so difficult? Grow up already, Antionette." Frustration was rising in her mother and Lucy knew that the argument was pointless. Her mother's mind was made up, and with it closed so tightly, there was no way she could convince her of something Lucy wasn't even sure she understood. How could her dad be dead, but here? Maybe she was living in a fantasy world. She knew it sounded crazy and only an open mind would be able to accept it. Lucy's mother's mind was as tightly closed as a storm cellar in the winter.

Later that night, Lucy sprawled on her bed staring at the ceiling. She was replaying the garden conversation with her mother from earlier. With a heavy sadness in her heart, Lucy knew what she must do. Depleted by her mother's obstinance, tired from the months and years living in opposition, and clueless of what it meant if she didn't, Lucy resigned herself to taking her mother's advice. To make her happy would make Lucy happy, and she only had one parent left to please, so she ought to be a good daughter and do just that.

12

PAINTING OUTSIDE THE LINES

Mae, 2022

Miles arrived at 7 a.m. sharp on Saturday morning, paint cans, brushes, rollers, and breakfast sandwiches in tow. Mae had barely awoken when the doorbell rang, and momentarily forgetting about their preset time for porch painting, was very confused to see a tall man in a backward cap wielding paint supplies eagerly awaiting her at the front door.

"You forgot," he conjectured with a jovial smile when she opened the door. Mae was in her pajamas, hair in a mess pulled on top of her head, rubbing the sandman's overnight gifts from one eye.

"No, no, I definitely remembered. I just wasn't aware that the proverbial bird needed to catch his worm *this* early," Mae replied, suddenly self-conscious of her appearance. She crossed her arms, hesitated a moment, then asked, "Is that bacon I smell?"

Miles' grin widened even further, "Applewood smoked bacon, gouda, and egg sandwiches for your early morning trouble." He held up a white paper bag proudly, the grease stains on which made her stomach growl.

Mae leaned into the doorframe, aware of her empty stomach and this breakfast angel before her. "Amazing. Come on inside and I'll start a pot of coffee and get changed."

Miles followed her in, leaving the painting supplies on the porch. He found himself a seat on a wooden chair at the small kitchen table while Mae fished a jar of coffee grounds out of the cabinet. She set a filter in the coffee maker, added water and grounds, then topped it off with a few dashes of cinnamon. She stole a glance at Miles, wondering if he was watching.

"Cinnamon? Look at you, you little barista," Miles teased.

"I am making coffee for the finest coffee maker in Cale Cove. I have to bring a little something extra to the table."

Miles appreciated the care Mae put into making the coffee special for him. She selected two mugs from the cabinet, set them on the counter, then retreated upstairs to change while the coffee was brewing. Miles sat alone in the kitchen, looking around at a room that was familiar to him, but newly different. He focused on a collection of three framed pieces that hung offset from each other on one wall. He stood to look at them closer—all dried flowers in various arrangements, sandwiched between two pieces of glass secured by a thin gold frame. They were delicate and understated but beautiful. Mae re-entered the room and saw what Miles was looking at.

"These are beautiful," he said.

"Oh…thank you. Kind of a long-lost hobby of mine," Mae responded.

"You put these together?" Miles asked.

"I did. Back when I lived in Chicago, I didn't have space for a garden, so every week when I'd grocery shop, I would buy myself a bouquet of flowers and a week or two later when they were past their prime, I pressed them between old textbooks and then made them into little pictures like this… voila!" Mae explained, gesturing to the wall's arrangement.

Miles contemplated each one carefully, taking in each tiny black-eyed Susan, petunia, daisy. "My mom was a gardener; she would have loved these," Miles seemed captivated by thought, so Mae waited for him to say more. "I think they're fantastic. You should do more now that you have a garden."

"The thought has crossed my mind. And then the guilt sets in of needing to find a job as a higher priority and I never get around to it," Mae laughed nervously. She returned to the counter where the coffee pot sat full of freshly brewed coffee and poured them each a mug. She added oat milk to her own and gestured with the carton to Miles.

"No thanks, I like mine black," he said, accepting his mug from her.

Mae suggested they go outside, so the two returned to the porch where they had sat when Miles suggested painting the porch initially. They sipped their coffee and ate their breakfast sandwiches in a comfortable silence, watching the birds flit from tree to tree, waving at the neighbors walking by with their dogs, and soaking in the early morning sun. Mae loved people who were at ease in silence, not needing to fill every space with idle chatter, and instead were able to enjoy their presence without expectation. Mae also loved summer mornings. Everything moved slower in the warm glow. The soft rays and overnight dew glistening on the grass made everything have a sparkling movie-scene quality. Summer mornings were a perfect time to read, sip coffee, and get lost in thought.

After they finished their breakfast, Miles prepared the painting supplies and they settled into a groove, picking up conversation while they painted. They talked about the cafe, and how Miles grew up in town. They talked about Mae's family and her job before the Great Upheaval (how Mae was internally referring to her sequential job and boyfriend loss, followed by moving to Cale Cove). After a minute or so of silence, Mae's curiosity got the best of her and she asked, "So, you said your mom is a gardener?"

"Was, yeah. She died when I was in high school," Miles stated matter-of-factly.

Mae dropped her brush and turned to Miles, holding his eye contact. "Miles, I'm so sorry that happened to you."

He laughed nervously, "Thanks. Yeah, I am, too. She was…" he thought for a moment, paused mid-brush stroke poised on a step ladder, "she was an incredible woman."

When he didn't say more but also didn't continue painting, Mae inquired, "Do you want to tell me about her?"

Miles looked struck. By what, Mae was unsure. For a split second she thought she had crossed a line and made him feel awkward. Just as she was wishing she could put the words back in her mouth and move on to lighter subjects, Miles smiled as if Mae had unlocked an opportunity he'd been waiting for. "I'd love to," he replied. Miles stepped down from the ladder and gently set his brush on the lid of the paint can. He sat next to Mae on the floor of the porch and began, "I know a lot of people kind of idealize dead loved ones like they were some sort of saint in their life, and I don't want to do that," he paused, "but honestly, she was."

Mae watched Miles' face light up with love, the corners of his eyes crinkling with each smile as he recounted his earliest memories of his mother. She was grateful to see this softer side of Miles. He told her of how he was the oldest of four boys and he and his mother always had a special relationship. While most parents leaned on the eldest sibling to help raise the younger ones, and Miles' mother did that to a certain extent, their relationship always remained separate from those with his siblings. Miles sat with her in the garden after school while she quizzed him for spelling tests, and she never missed a single tee ball—and then later, baseball—game. Long past the age when other boys in his class became embarrassed of their mothers, Miles never did.

"Every time I'd bring home a report card that was straight A's, we'd go to Digby's Dogs to celebrate," he smiled at the memory.

"Those Chicago dogs are DIVINE," Mae said emphatically, having recently experienced Cale Cove's hot dog haven.

"Truly the best." Miles recounted, "There was this one time, I think I was in maybe 6th grade, and it was the end of the school year, so everyone had this excited, buzzing energy about them. Our report cards hadn't come out yet, but I knew what my grades were going to be. Not only did we get Digby's Dogs, but my mom planned this whole afternoon of mini golf, go karts, and ice cream cake with all my friends, just to celebrate the end of the year. She arranged it with all of the moms beforehand and picked us up from school for the surprise. It was so awesome."

"She sounds like a fun mom," Mae offered.

"She was. But she was also serious. I mean, she taught me about serious things. My dad's an attorney so he worked a lot and wasn't around a whole lot growing up. I think I learned work ethic and integrity from him, but my mom taught me about people. How to listen to them, relate to them, care for them. It wasn't until I went to college that I started to realize not everyone is taught empathy and how to honor their emotions."

"You must miss her a lot," Mae lamented.

"I do. Time is a weird thing with death. They found her cancer in a late stage, so life seemed to happen at warp speed initially. For months she just got sicker and sicker and eventually stopped getting out of bed and then nurses came in to make sure she was comfortable and not in pain. During those months I just wanted time to slow down because I knew what was coming. I wanted to memorize everything about her and commit every detail to my memory.

"But then at the same time I saw she was tired. She fought a losing battle with cancer and her body was depleted, so I also wanted time to disappear for her so that she could be out of pain. Then she died and time froze. I was stuck in this black hole of loss while the world around me moved on.

I remember the day after she died, I went to the grocery store to get something my dad needed for dinner. I paid for it and the checkout lady said something like 'Have a good day!' and I'm sure I murmured something in return, but it was so surreal. She had no idea that my mom just died. I had just watched the most significant person in my life take her last breath and we were sitting here acting like life was as mundane as buying a head of broccoli. It seemed so cruel that time would keep moving forward and not give me even a second to figure out how to feel. But eventually I was glad it moved forward because I didn't want to be stuck in that place of loss either. Then before you know it, it's been 15 years."

"My God, Miles. That must have been so hard for you," Mae said, furrowing her brow in sympathy. She couldn't help but think of Lucy's death. While Lucy wasn't her parent and she lived to a beautiful old age, she could relate well to the sinking feeling of grief.

"It was. It's definitely a formative thing at that age," Miles replied. He fidgeted with the brush for a moment, then said, "Thanks for letting me share that with you."

"Of course. I'm glad you did," Mae offered him a compassionate smile. "I uh...I lost my grandmother a few years ago and it's tough. It's different, I know, but..."

"Loss is loss, Mae. I'm sorry you had to go through that," Miles said sincerely.

"Life is loss, isn't it?" Mae replied.

Miles' eyebrows raised in surprise at Mae's frankness but considered the sentiment. "Yeah, I guess it is. But it's also newness, and growth," he offered with a shrug.

Mae's mind was on the garden and her conversations there with Lucy. She desperately wanted to tell Miles but thought it could be harsh knowing she could talk to her grandmother and his mom was still gone. She put it out of her mind and raised her paintbrush, "To new friendships!"

Miles touched his paintbrush to hers midair and laughed in return, "To new friendships."

They spent the rest of the morning painting, Mae working on the railing and Miles on the ceiling. When the morning sun rose higher in the sky, they moved on to the floor of the porch, each with a roller in hand. Mae was always barefoot, and Miles joined her in removing his shoes when they started painting the floor. Miles worked carefully and Mae enjoyed watching the precision with which he endeavored every movement. She never had patience for such rigor and was much more liberal with her rolling technique.

While Miles cut carefully around the edge of where the porch met the house, Mae continued rolling the floor freely next to him until she rolled over the side of his foot. While she was sure it was accidental, she wouldn't mind if her subconscious mind made her do it on purpose now that she was looking at Miles' amused surprise in response. He stopped his roller and stood, mouth agape, staring at Mae. Mae giggled in response.

"You're out of control," Miles jested.

"It goes too slowly the way you're doing it." Mae continued rolling, this time definitely intentionally painting Miles' foot into the porch. He set his roller against the house and Mae's giggles erupted, rendering her doubled over in laughter. Miles strode over to the paint bucket and picked up the brush he had placed there earlier.

"While we're at it, I think you missed a spot here," Miles said while lightly tapping the wet brush to the tip of Mae's nose. She shrieked and laughed uncontrollably at cool, calm, and collected Miles now participating in her game. She rolled the paint up his shin in response, then dropped the roller and ran into the yard, avoiding any repercussions.

"You're cut off!" Miles yelled, following her into the yard, paintbrush in hand. He caught her in the backyard and slung an arm around her waist, lifting her up over his shoulder like he was carrying a bag of sand. Mae squealed in protest as Miles painted her foot with the brush his other hand carried.

Mae laugh-screamed, "Truce! Truce! I call a truce!"

Miles put her back on the ground and she stumbled into a seat with her legs out in front of her. Miles joined her on the grass laughing. "Interesting time to call a truce when you're unarmed," he said, holding his paintbrush as a sword in a defensive position.

Mae raised her index fingers in a cross in front of her and pleaded, "Back! No more!"

Miles dropped the brush in the grass and put his hands up in mock arrest. "Alright, alright, it's a truce." The two sat laughing, holding each other's eyes while they did. Miles moved in closer to Mae, raised one paint-covered hand, and tucked a loose strand of hair behind Mae's ear. She stopped laughing and rested in a smile, connected with Miles's eyes.

Miles said softly, "Have dinner with me tomorrow."

Mae nodded, grinning. "Okay," she said, "but leave the paint here?"

"Deal," Miles replied. He stole a glance at his watch and realized it was already time to walk Buster. "As much as I hate for this session of body painting to end, there's a rowdy little rapscallion next door needing my walking services."

Miles and Mae picked up the paint supplies and admired their work. They had nearly finished! Miles left and met Patty and Buster on the porch next door for their afternoon walk, and after taking stock of all the paint on Miles, Patty looked next door at Mae still on the porch, paint drying on her own nose. Patty gave her a knowing wink before returning inside her home. Mae cleaned herself up and later met up with Cassie to fill her in on the day's unfolding.

Cassie squealed. She was lying on her back on a park bench overlooking the lake while Mae was sitting next to her in the grass, fidgeting with a few blades, braiding them between her fingers. A wistful smile hadn't left Mae's face since recounting the morning to Cassie.

"I can't believe he asked you out!" Cassie exclaimed. "Shy, cool Miles Robertson makes his move."

"He doesn't do this a lot, the dating thing?" Mae asked.

"No, not at all," Cassie thought for a moment, "I think the last time Miles had a girlfriend was in college. He usually dates someone for a little bit, but nothing really sticks."

"Well, we will see," Mae said, smiling into her grass braid.

13

ALL GOOD THINGS COME TO AN END

Lucy, 1958

The weeks that followed the garden conversation and Lucy's surrender to her mother's desires went by in a blur. She felt present only physically, often wondering if it was her life for which she was actively making choices or merely someone else's she was bearing witness to. She accepted Kurt's proposal and while she didn't feel butterflies or excitement the way she imagined she would, she knew he would be a good husband and father and an excellent son-in-law. Maybe she wasn't in head-over-heels Hollywood love, but she could certainly do worse. The primary thing that reassured Lucy that her decision was the right one, and the main reason for making it in the first place, was her mother's delight in becoming a mother of the bride.

Her elation at her new role in life gave Lucy's mother a lightened step, a joyous chatter, and the glow of confidence of someone no longer marred or identified by what she had lost, but who instead shone with the promise of what they had to look forward to. Her friends gushed about the wedding plans and predictions of how soon grandchildren might come. Lucy was committed to doing everything the way that her mother wanted it. Her mother had been through enough and if Lucy had the power to make any little detail of her life better, happier, she was willing to do it, because that is how much she loved her mother.

Lucy watched her mother's face carefully as she tried on wedding gowns, looking for clues to which one her mother preferred, then decided she too liked that one. The flowers she chose for the wedding—white calla lilies—were also her mother's favorite. She even let slide her mother's underhanded comments on "fitting into her dress" while Lucy indulged in cake samples at the bakery. They were to have a quaint backyard ceremony. This was the one detail Lucy desired and was subsequently glad her mother was also amenable to. The thought of her father's absence as she walked down the aisle alone felt like a boulder sunk deep in her stomach, made lighter only by the thought that his carefully curated garden would lay as backdrop to the nuptials. Lucy was sure she wouldn't see her father that day because of his quick disappearance when her mother's presence was known in the garden, but knowing that the ethereal garden where he was always waiting behind a thin veil of perceived reality provided Lucy with a comfort like nothing else.

The wedding was on a beautiful fall day. The afternoon sun, filtered through the newly golden and orange maple leaves, warmed the guests enough that they were grateful for the crisp evening air's arrival as the party was winding down. Lucy was a wild mix of emotions. She was glad to see her mother happy, but ambivalent about moving away with her new husband. Anxious about her new role as a wife. Sad to be leaving the place where she grew up and the garden where she reconnected with her late father. After the nuptials were said, the food eaten, and all the dances danced, Lucy's mother bid the last straggling guests goodbye. Lucy asked for a few minutes alone in the garden, and Kurt granted her the request.

Lucy sat on the bench, still in her wedding dress, and closed her eyes. She thought of her father and how she wished he could have been present for her wedding. She imagined how he might look all cleaned up in a suit, hair neatly combed, probably parted to the side the way he did when he went to church on Sunday mornings. The thought of her father's calloused hands and casual demeanor wrapped up in a suit and tie, dressed in his wedding best, gave her heart levity.

"I was here, kiddo, and it was beautiful," came the deep, familiar voice. "*You* are beautiful. Kurt is quite a lucky man."

Lucy smiled and opened her eyes. John was looking at her with the biggest smile, watery eyes full of love and pride in his eldest daughter. Lucy soaked it in, but just as quickly as her happiness arrived at seeing her dad, sorrow flashed over her face and sunk into her stomach. Kurt had recently finished school to become a pastor and accepted a job that would be taking them to the next state over. Away from the home where she grew up, away from her father's magical garden. Lucy had to tell her dad this; she had to say goodbye all over again and she couldn't bear to do it, so she didn't.

14

SPILLING THE TEA

Mae, 2022

"Now I know I'm the iced tea queen of Cale Cove, but you, Mae, seem to be campaigning for the title of lemonade queen with this." Patty drank a long sip from the straw in her dewy glass of lemonade. Swallowing, she closed her eyes and tilted her head back, fully enjoying it. "*Mmm mm mm*, Mae, this is *good*."

Mae laughed and replied, "I'm so glad you like it! I cannot claim ownership though, this is all Lucy."

"No kidding?" Patty replied, now smacking her lips at the latent tartness.

Mae watched her in amusement. "Yep. She always had fresh lemonade and warm chocolate chip cookies at the ready. The coziest grandma of all grandmas. Hey, can I ask you about her?"

"Shoot," replied Patty, taking another sip.

"Why do you think I didn't know that she was born here in Cale Cove? I mean I didn't know, neither did my mom…it just doesn't make sense to me. Why would that be a secret worth keeping?"

Patty mulled over the question and thought for several moments, crafting her response. "Well, as I told you the other day, we were very close in our childhood here. Then this big catastrophic thing happened—her dad dying—and then her best friend left. If I had to guess, I think maybe she felt abandoned and perhaps decided when she married and moved with Kurt that she'd start a new life in a way." Patty shrugged at her hypothesis.

Mae considered this and supposed it made sense. She tried to imagine creating a new life from here on out in her own life, a life in Cale Cove. While she was at least ten years older than Lucy was when she did it, she supposed she could see the appeal. "There was so much heartbreak to leave behind," Mae said, no more to Patty than to herself.

"Exactly," Patty concurred.

Mae remembered the locket just then and fished it out of her pocket. She had cleaned it up since the first day of finding it, and even though the clasp still functioned perfectly well, she still hadn't felt comfortable wearing it, so it rode around in her pocket every day like a hidden sidekick. She held it in her hand, admiring the metallic flash in the sun. She turned it over and again looked at the initials carved in an elaborate script, *LAM*.

Mae turned to Patty and stuck out her cupped hand. "Patty, do you think *L-A-M* could be Lucinda Antoinette Monroe?"

Patty's face contorted in confusion, furrowing her brow while she looked at Mae's hand, then suddenly recognition dawned on her. "My heavens, Mae, where did you get this?!"

"I found it in the garden one day, half buried in the dirt. I've been carrying it around since and put it in the back of my mind until you told me Lucy grew up here in Cale Cove. I thought it would be crazy and far-fetched, but thought *maybe?* Maybe those in initials could be hers."

"Oh honey, yes. This is her locket! I remember the day her daddy gave that to her…" Patty trailed off, wondering if she'd said too much.

"Patty…if this is Grandma Lucy's locket, and I found it in this house's backyard, does that mean, this house…?"

"Was where she grew up, yes," Patty replied with tears in her eyes. "The Monroes were here and the Janneys, my family, were right next door, where I live now. Earl and I moved back to help with my mother at the end of her life," her voice grew quiet, not needing to tell her full story. "Anyway, yes, honey. This was your Grandma Lucy's house."

Mae turned the necklace over in her hands, finding new, nostalgic value in its delicate chain and beautifully etched edges. "L-A-M," she said to herself, "Lucinda Antoinette Monroe." A piece of her grandmother in her hands again. She couldn't escape the feeling that finding the necklace in the garden where Lucy posthumously appeared and talked to her was more than a mere coincidence. Mae's mind was reeling. Lucy was here. Her childhood was here. Up until recently, she thought this town was a mythical place and then suddenly it was on a map, and she was here and *here* in her grandmother's childhood home. It was almost too much to make sense of.

"Patty, I have to tell you something and you must withhold judgment. I swear to you I am not crazy, though I definitely considered it when what I'm about to tell you happened…" Mae hesitated, "but I trust you to believe me," Mae said in all seriousness. Her eyes pleaded with Patty to stay with her, to hear her out.

"Of course, honey, I don't think you're crazy. What is it you have to tell me?"

"I've seen Lucy. Here."

Patty's eyes narrowed and head cocked to the side. "I don't follow. Like a ghost?"

"Not exactly," Mae considered how to explain it, then decided exactly how it happened was best. She told Patty about the day she was working in the garden, the third anniversary of Lucy's passing, and she missed her greatly. She told her how she fell asleep on the ground and how she talked to Lucy, and she thought it was a dream, but when she opened her eyes, she was still there. She told her what Lucy looked like (exactly how she remembered her), how she sounded, what they talked about. It was all the same as before but made no sense and had no place in reality. But it was real. "It was real, Patty, I swear. As real as you and me sitting here talking now." Mae continued, recounting the conversations she'd had since then and how the garden, already a delightful backyard escape, was now her favorite place to be because it meant spending time with her beloved grandmother again.

Mae asked, "Remember the other day when you brought over those lemon cookies and iced tea? I was with Lucy that day! She disappeared right as you walked up though."

Patty was taking all of this in, her face devoid of judgment. She considered everything Mae told her and a slow, small smile crept over her lips. She nodded knowingly at Mae and said, "Oh, I believe you, honey. The magic of the garden has returned."

Patty's response was the last thing Mae had imagined. Brush her off and tell her she was dreaming? Yes. Question her sanity and make an excuse to go home immediately? Perhaps. Commit her to a mental hospital? Likely. Not only believing her but alluding to prior knowledge of the power of the garden; now *that* was far-fetched. "You've *known* about this? How?" Mae inquired.

"I've known of it, yes. Truth be told, I'd almost forgotten about it, it's been so long since…" Patty trailed off.

"Since what?"

"Well, it was when we were teenagers, after Lucy's daddy died. That garden was his pride and joy, and he had a marvelous green thumb. Oh, if you could see what it looked like then…magnificent. Though you've done a wonderful job with it now. Lucy found a certain catharsis in working it after his death. She'd been depressed for some time, rightfully so, and the garden had gotten overgrown. When she started working in it, I think she found a closeness to her father that she didn't know she needed. Proximity to his legacy, perhaps. Until it was proximity to *him*.

"She kept it to herself for a while, of course, because she probably felt how you're feeling right now, not sure if anyone would believe her. Especially soon after losing someone so significant in your life, grief colors everything. Lucy knew it sounded far-fetched to be talking to her deceased father, but I witnessed the peace that it gave her. When she told me about it, I had no choice but to believe her. She was my best friend and I trusted her more than anything or anyone in the world. Sure, I thought it was wild, but life is wild, you know? Who do we think we are going around thinking we really understand anything about, well, anything? And she had proof!"

Mae was surprised, "What do you mean, proof?"

"The proof lies in your hand right there," Patty replied. Mae's hand instinctively closed around the locket in her hand, then she opened it again, gazing upon it with new eyes. Patty continued, "When she told me about the garden conversations with her daddy, Lucy showed me that necklace. John gave it to her, telling her it was for her 18th birthday, which of course, he wasn't alive for. He had purchased it previously and never got the chance to give it to her. Lucy thought she was dreaming when all of this happened because that was the most likely explanation for conversing with a dead loved one, but when she awoke and it started raining, she retreated to the house. She told me once she was inside and processing the conversation, she noticed that the necklace was still around her neck."

Goosebumps chilled over Mae's arms, "It wasn't a dream."

"It wasn't a dream," Patty replied in agreement. "So, imagine my surprise when I see you with this locket that my teenage best friend received as a gift from her dead father decades ago in a garden you have been rehabbing for fun." Patty laughed at it all. "It's wonderfully absurd and just so delightful."

"Wonderfully absurd," Mae agreed, "What a great phrase." Then she changed the subject, "Were you at Lucy's funeral? That day was such a blur of family and friends and a lot of people I didn't know…"

"I was, yes. It was a beautiful service, and your eulogy was just wonderful. You really captured Lucy's essence and I'm sure she would have been so proud."

Mae blinked away a threatening tear in the corner of her eye. "Thank you, Patty. That means a lot to me." Patty leaned over and gave Mae's hand a squeeze, then redirected her attention to a smartly dressed Miles making his way up the sidewalk with a picnic basket in hand.

15

THREE'S A CROWD

Mae, 2022

"Oh my gosh, it's that time already?!" Mae exclaimed. "Miles, I'm so sorry, we were chatting, and I totally lost track of time. Give me five minutes." Mae rushed inside in a flurry.

"Not a problem, take your time!" Miles called after her. He replaced her in the seat next to Patty, smoothing his shorts as he sat. He was wearing a dark blue, short-sleeved, button-down shirt, crisply pressed gray shorts, and bright white sneakers. He had traded his signature disheveled mop under a baseball cap for well-styled locks.

"Well, don't you look handsome," Patty winked. "Taking my girl on a picnic, I see."

Miles flushed and nodded, trying to hide his nerves, "Don't tease. You know I haven't done this in a while."

Patty chuckled to herself, "I know, honey, and I think it's sweet. I'm not teasing at all."

Inside, Mae changed into her white denim shorts and light blue seersucker tank with little yellow flowers on it. She splashed cool water on her face and applied mascara, blush, and lip balm. She released her hair out of its unruly braid and combed through it with her fingers, letting the waves fall past her shoulders. After sliding her feet into her flat leather sandals, she was ready to go. Walking back downstairs to the porch, she caught a moment of conversation between Miles and Patty before pushing open the door.

"I know there's no strict timeline on it, but now that we know, wouldn't it be better done sooner rather than later? I don't want her to know we've known and have been keeping it from her."

"Of course. I'll make sure my dad gets the paperwork ready as soon as possible."

"Paperwork for what?" Mae asked breezily, re-entering the porch.

"Wow, look at you!" Patty exclaimed. Both Miles and Mae looked at her. "Right, sorry, this is your time. You kids have fun!" Patty waved as she walked back to her own house, leaving Miles and Mae laughing to themselves.

"She speaks the truth though, Mae. Wow." Mae smiled and placed her hand in Miles' outstretched hand.

"Thank you," she replied, playfully rolling her eyes as he spun her around for a 360 view. "Ready?" Miles nodded with a smile and the two headed off to the park in the center of the quaint downtown.

The park was a vast green space nestled in between three streets—Main St., Lake St., and Madison St. While the locals referred to the park as "the square," its configuration was really a triangle, shaped by the grassy void of the three streets, surrounded by buildings more than a hundred years old. Once banks and city government buildings, they now housed boutiques, hair salons, restaurants, Cassie's brewpub, The Crooked Cask, and of course, Miles' Cove Coffee. The park was beautifully shaded by ancient oak and shagbark hickory trees, offering not only a cool reprieve from summer heat, but a charming and cozy shroud, much like an adult fort naturally made by the colossal trees.

When they arrived, Miles set out a blanket he removed from the basket and gestured for Mae to sit down. He pulled out chicken salad, croissants, sliced fruit, and a bottle of wine with two plastic cups. "I hope this is OK?"

"Of course it is!" Mae reassured Miles, pouring her a cup of wine.

Once he poured his own, Miles held up his in a toast, proposing, "To beginnings."

"To beginnings," Mae repeated.

As the two had dinner, the conversation flowed from their similar interest in books and music to their lives growing up and their favorite parts of Cale Cove. "Did you ever want to move away from here? It felt like when I was growing up, nobody wanted to end up in the town they grew up in," Mae asked.

"I did, actually. I left for college out of state and lived there for five or so years after graduation. I came back here when I burnt out from that job and the building where Cove Coffee is now went up for sale. It was always my dream to own a small business back home and it just felt like all the stars aligned when they did to bring me back here." Miles took a sip of wine, then continued, "I was burnt out from my job as a tax auditor—just brain numbingly dull work—my relationship had just ended, and the building was up for sale. Cale Cove didn't have a coffee spot at the time, and well," he paused to gesture at the downtown surrounding the park, "how can you have a town this charming without coffee?"

"You absolutely cannot," Mae agreed.

"How 'bout you?" Miles asked, "Did you always want to get away from the town you grew up in?"

"Oh gosh yes," Mae said without hesitation, "Birchfield is just a suburban wasteland." She laughed nervously. "There are places like Cale Cove—small, charming, something you might expect if a Richard Scarry book sprung to life—and then there are places like Chicago—big, bustling, variety, and whatever you could possibly want to eat and do nearby—and then there's Birchfield. It has busy streets and huge intersections everywhere, rendering it virtually unwalkable.

You have to drive everywhere. There's so much traffic and going to what? Every chain store you can imagine from restaurants to hardware to shopping, it's all chains. Absolutely zero personality, charm, or character. But people are somehow convinced they want to live there because the schools are highly rated and everyone else seems to think it's the dream."

"Oh no," Miles laughed. "I had no idea you felt so strongly, but I can see what you mean. I'm not a huge fan of the suburbs myself. So, you're feeling more settled here, in Cale Cove? Or do you miss the city?"

"I think I miss parts of it, like being able to get really good sushi at 10 p.m., but honestly, I like Cale Cove far more than I imagined I might. It's got a little something special here."

"Oh yeah?" Miles reclined on an elbow, flashing his bright smile that made Mae's stomach flutter.

"Yeah. Its residents have been quite welcoming, as I'm sure you can imagine."

Miles traced circles with his index finger on Mae's knee. He avoided her stare out of shyness, but his smile remained. His voice came out softer now, "We do like to make sure everyone here feels welcome." He met her eyes and for a moment; Mae didn't let her flushed cheeks embarrass her and sunk into the pleasure of Miles' finger delicately brushing her skin. His eyes looked down as he moved his face toward hers and she closed her eyes.

"Well, hey there folks!" The two shot apart, resuming their seats, separate, on the blanket. "Mind if I join you?" Before either Miles or Mae could say anything, Jim was folding his walking sticks and setting them in the grass next to the picnic and joining them on the blanket.

"Hey, Jim. What a surprise," Miles said flatly.

"I was just out walking on this fine evening and saw some people in the park. I walked closer and thought 'Hey, I know them!' so I had to come over. What a great idea, a picnic! My wife and I used to like picnics, I think," Jim hesitated, "That seems like something we used to do."

Whatever annoyance Mae felt upon Jim's party crashing dissipated with compassion at Jim's spotty memory. She couldn't imagine having an entire life with someone and then not being able to recall the small, lovely moments, like having a picnic in the park. She offered him some fruit. "Grapes, Jim?" She held the container up for him.

"Oh, I'd love some! You know grapes are my favorite fruit…" he trailed off while eating several. Mae looked at Miles, who was looking at her, and they both tried to hide their smirks.

"Hey, that's a flower!" Jim pointed at Mae's outstretched arm, where a tiny bouquet was tattooed.

"Oh yeah, I got that as a little memorial for my grandma Lucy. It's—"

"No wait. Don't tell me! I know this." Jim scrunched his brow in firm concentration as he tried to come up with the name of the flower on Mae's wrist. After several moments he gave up, "Gah, I don't remember. What is it?"

"It's lavender."

"Lavender! Of course it is. I used to know the names of all kinds of flowers."

"Oh really?" Mae was interested.

"Yeah, when I worked," Jim replied.

"Did you do landscaping?" Miles asked.

"Yeah, kind of. Well, we took the," Jim gestured an imaginary shape of something with his hands, "and you know arranged it with the…then you put it all together, and, you know." They didn't know, but Jim seemed satisfied with the explanation, so they went with it.

"That's cool, Jim. Did you know Mae here is a resident gardening expert?" Miles asked.

"No!" Jim elated, "You have a garden, Mae?"

"Miles is overselling. It's just kind of been a hobby since I moved here, restoring this garden to what it maybe once was. It's this cool space that just looks like it's been overgrown for years, maybe decades. But underneath it all is super rich soil and there's even a bench already in there," Mae explained. She couldn't help but wonder about the magical quality of the garden. If she could talk to Lucy in it, could other people talk to Lucy, too?

After what started as a picnic for two ended as a picnic for three, Miles walked Mae home with Jim on her other side. Mae knew they'd laugh about this tomorrow and wonder how Jim could be so oblivious even while walking her home that he was crashing a date, but they both didn't mind it one bit. When they reached her doorstep, she hugged them both goodbye, kissing only Miles on the cheek. Falling asleep that night, she couldn't help but think that no matter how quirky and unexpected, that was quite possibly the best first date she'd ever had.

16

MILES MEETS THE GARDEN

Mae, 2022

Later that week, Mae was working the garden in the afternoon, cursing herself for not getting out there earlier in the day. The sun had risen high in the sky, shrouded by not a single cloud. Its rays were hot on her shoulders, but she needed to harvest the fast-growing tomatoes before they split at the seams and rid the garden of the weeds that grew like, well, weeds, new ones ostensibly appearing before her eyes.

"Hey there, young lady," came Miles' smooth voice.

Mae propped her hand at her forehead creating a visor from the sun so she could see her garden visitor more clearly. "Hey there," she said with a big smile.

"I come bearing hibiscus iced tea; I thought you might need it on a day like today," Miles set the two iced and sweating cups from the cafe on the bench and lowered to a seat, waiting for Mae.

"You're a lifesaver. It's brutal out here today." A locust's loud chirp added to the scorched ambience. Mae joined him on the bench and thanked him for the beverage. The first sip chilled her from the inside out and felt like diving into a pool of bliss on the punishingly hot day.

"So, the other night..." Miles started.

Mae laughed, shaking her head, "was unexpected," she finished.

Miles was laughing now, too. "Oh, you didn't know I invited Jim, too? Should have been clearer."

"It was perfect," Mae said sincerely. "Jim or no Jim."

"I concur," Miles agreed, taking a long sip from the straw. "So, what have you got going on back here?" Miles looked around the vast herbal-vegetable-floral jungle that surrounded them.

"Oh! Well..." Mae guided Miles on a tour of the garden, starting with the rows of vegetables she was harvesting today. She continued on to tell him about the herbs she'd planted, basil being her favorite so far because it made the best pesto, and ended with the perennials she'd since been able to identify that surrounded the patch. Miles was impressed. After he offered to help pull the daily weeds, Mae went inside to get him a pair of gloves to guard against the spiny thistles and at once he was alone in the space. He sat on the bench, and while he waited for Mae, he imagined what his mother would say about this garden. Her garden. It had been years since it looked this good, but he remembered, it did once. Miles inhaled the faint smell of basil deeply and let the air flow slowly out his nostrils as his shoulders relaxed.

Inside, Mae found the spare pair of gloves instantly, but detoured to the kitchen for a glass of water. When her phone dinged on the counter, she got pulled into reading an email update from her cousin Emily who was sailing around the world with her boyfriend, Theo. They were currently in Japan and the email painted a wonderful picture of the last week of their travels. Mae finished reading the email and paused to look at Miles in the garden before she returned outside. He was sitting on the bench, his head hung low. He wiped at his eyes and Mae realized he was crying, but he was also... talking? Who was he talking to? The realization hit Mae like the icy water of the first lake plunge of the season, stealing her breath and sending shivers through her limbs. She dillydallied several more minutes inside before returning to Miles in the garden.

When she walked up, Miles had a wide smile and wet eyelashes. She approached with tentative presence, requesting silently if her return was OK with him. "Mae…" he started.

"I think I know what you're going to tell me, and I want you to know I believe you," Mae interrupted. She held Miles' gaze to let him know she was serious and that made his bottom lip puff out. He bit it and swallowed back tears.

"My mom…" he started. Mae nodded, taking him into her arms and hugging him for a long time. "How did you know?" he asked.

"Because I met my grandma Lucy the same way. I was out here gardening alone and thinking of her and then she was there, clear as day, as if she wasn't even…"

"Dead," Miles finished. "It doesn't make any sense."

"I know it doesn't."

"Have you talked to your grandma more than once?"

Mae sat back and smiled, "several times."

"Wow," Miles replied.

They sat in silence absorbing what they each now knew to be true. Of course, they had each experienced the magic of the garden and felt it true in their heart, but isn't there always that little bit of you that holds back on affirming your truth until it is seen and acknowledged by someone else? Humans are funny creatures like that. Their pain and their love need to be witnessed before they will allow it to be real.

Mae noticed atop a branch of the oak tree at the side of the yard sat a bird with a striking blue tail feather, watching them with precision, a female blue jay. She swore she even saw its head move back and forth between her and Miles when they exchanged conversation. They continued to work in the garden, sharing with each other what Mae's grandmother and Miles' mother had meant to them. Their losses were different as their relationships to their beloved were different, but all loss cuts deep. The grief that filled the space was profound, and with that in common, they could relate to the profundity of speaking to them again after years of mortality-imposed silence.

The mood lightened as their work continued. Mae tightened her grip on a final thistle, a strong one that extended deep in the soil. When she gave it a firm tug, it didn't budge. She added a second hand to it, grounded her stance and pulled hard. The weed gave way and with it, flung chunks of dirt through the air and all over Miles crouching in the garden beside it. Mae froze, watching his dirt-covered face in shock.

"I am SO sorry…"

Miles blinked the dirt out of his eyes, spit some from his mouth, and shook his head to rustle it out of his hair. "Always the instigator, aren't you?" He picked the weed off the pile and threw it back to Mae, hitting her in the elbow and leaving a clump of dirt stuck to her dampened skin, trails of it dropping down her arm. She squealed and stepped several paces back from Miles, laughing while she wiped the dirt off.

"Truce, truce! I call a truce! I did not mean to start a war this time!" she belted out between laughs. Miles strode toward her and Mae's eyes flashed concern for a second, then excited knowing. He wrapped his arms around her waist and pulled her in for a long-awaited kiss. Mae was laughing at first, then settled into his soft, gentle lips.

"Truce accepted," he said.

"Wow," she whispered.

"I've been wanting to do that," replied Miles, blushing now. They kissed again, lingering for a moment, then parted.

Miles cleared his throat. "Should we uh…continue?" he gestured to the garden.

Mae couldn't wipe the smile from her face and didn't want to. "Of course."

They settled back into pulling weeds, placing them on the weed pile where Mae had started stacking them to dry out in the sun, and harvesting the vegetables that were ready. After a while, Miles stopped pulling weeds and suggested, "We should dig a koi pond in here."

    Mae laughed. "You know who said the *exact* same thing? Lucy."

17

POND PLANS PLANTED

Mae, 2022

A week passed and Mae hadn't heard much from Miles, so she was surprised when he reignited the idea of a koi pond when he texted her on Thursday.

"I have off on Sunday. How 'bout digging that pond then?" he asked.

"Sounds good!" Mae replied.

All of their conversations had been short lately and Mae was beginning to wonder if she did something wrong. The picnic dinner was great and the kiss in the garden later that week was amazing. She thought they were starting something, and she really liked him. But then Miles began to pull back and used the age old "work is really busy right now" excuse. She tried not to think much of it, and instead looked forward to seeing him again for their pond creation collaboration.

The section of garden they chose for the koi pond was a large, unwieldy area. For whatever reason, Mae hadn't yet touched the section in the corner by the cement bench, mostly because she hadn't needed to. There was so much space that had already been revived to a growing space for her vegetables, herbs, and flowers, that she simply hadn't needed to touch this particular plot of land. She was now glad that she didn't because it introduced the perfect location for a koi pond. Miles had planned it all out and while she was expecting him to arrive the next day with the necessary supplies, she decided to get a head start on digging out the area. She found it surprisingly easy to dig as she worked through the day. There were no trees nearby so while digging two feet into the earth should have been difficult, she didn't run into many roots that her shovel couldn't cut through and handle.

As soon as Mae had reached the desired depth, she discovered something peculiar. She reached down into the earth and pulled at what appeared to be a liner already placed. She continued digging to the desired level all across the pond area, and sure enough, the liner extended precisely everywhere she had marked and dug for the pond. It was ripped and tattered as though it had been there for many years and would surely need to come up before placing the new one down, but she left it in place to show Miles.

The next day, Miles had his associate, Jake, cover the coffee shop, so he arrived early with all the necessary koi pond materials: liner, filter, aerator, and a truck bed full of rocks. When Mae showed him the existing liner, albeit in its tattered form, he too was surprised.

"How weird is that?" he said. "We planned a koi pond exactly where one already existed?"

"Unless the liner could be something else?" Mae pondered.

Either way, they decided they needed to remove it to make way for the new one. They worked all day and evening on the hole that Mae had started the previous day, laying down the new liner and smoothing it perfectly, securing it with rocks around the edges, and adding rocks for visual interest to the bottom of the pond, and also, Mae noted silently, for her new fish friends to have a place to hide from the large birds that seemed to patrol the area. After they laid the liner, Miles dragged the garden hose all the way to the backyard and planted it in the newly dug pond.

"We'll have to test the pH once the water is filled," he instructed.

"But now we wait," Mae replied, watching the hose water fill the pond.

"Now we wait," Miles echoed, taking a seat beside the pond.

After several minutes of watching the pond fill in silence, Miles asked, "Hey, Mae?" she looked over at him expecting more. "Do you mind if I have a little bit here…alone?"

Mae knew he was asking to talk to his mother again without asking directly. "Yes, of course," she replied, understanding his need to see his mother again. She stood, brushing the dirt from the back of her legs and straightening her shorts. When Mae left the garden, Miles felt a heaviness in his chest.

He liked Mae, but just like many women before her, he felt himself sabotaging his own feelings before they were even allowed to grow. He knew the root of it was the fear of loss, but even knowing so didn't prevent him from doing it. He exhaled a sound of frustration. "What is *wrong* with me?"

"Absolutely nothing," came a gentle female voice.

"Mom…" Miles' eyes were immediately damp.

"You're scared," she said.

"I know."

"But you can't keep avoiding love, Miles, you have so much to give," she continued.

Miles considered how to verbalize the weight of emotion in his chest. His mother waited patiently as he absentmindedly pulled at a loose thread on the hem of his shirt and twirled it around his finger. Finally, he said, "Love is loss." He swallowed hard. "I can't go through another loss like yours. It was too hard. Even fifteen years later, it's still so hard." Miles swiped at his damp eyelashes with each thumb. He closed his eyes and took a deep breath to steady it. "I miss you, mom. I miss your advice and your presence. I miss how no matter what you were doing you would drop it to listen to me and make me feel like what I had to say was the most important thing you had to listen to that day."

"I'm still here, honey, like I told you before. Not just in this garden but in your heart, always. You can always talk to me, and I will listen. But if I'm being honest, I don't think losing me is the only thing holding you back from Mae."

Miles groaned in acknowledgement. "Nicole," he said.

"That was a loss, too, Miles, whether you see it that way or not," she said gently.

"I broke up with her though. We outgrew each other. She didn't die," he said.

"Not all loss is death, sweetheart. You two were together for a long time. The deeper the love, the harder the fall, and first loves always seem to fall hard."

"Yeah," Miles contemplated. "I think maybe I thought we had to stay together because she knew you and I couldn't imagine being with someone you didn't meet. It didn't seem right. But we weren't right for each other."

"I think you were right for each other for a time. I was glad you had her to lean on when my time had come, but not all relationships are meant to last forever," his mother explained.

"Exactly my point," Miles said. "Exactly why I can feel myself pulling away from Mae. I don't want to, but you're right, I'm scared. What if it also ends?"

"Then you will have memories of the wonderful times you had together. Nothing is guaranteed, Miles, nothing. But when you're given a moment or a time with someone you care for, don't rob yourself of the fullest joy it can bring by denying your heart's desire."

They sat next to each other, Miles contemplating what to say next. He felt instantly better being in the presence of his mother again, but his thoughts were with Mae. "I like her, mom. I like her a lot."

"I know."

"That scares the shit out of me."

"I know," she nodded, still watching him.

"So, what do I do?" Miles asked. He gazed not at his mother, but at their reflection in the pool of rising water. His face distorted with rhythmic ripples as the hose constantly ran into it, but he could still see his mother beside him.

"Miles," she started gently, "your heart contains multitudes," she paused. "Love is an infinite force throttled only by your willingness to let it flow through you. Love never runs out. It never stops."

Miles received his mother's words and felt a flutter in his stomach, in his heart, when he thought of what it would mean to allow himself love. He explored the feeling then admitted softly aloud, "I'm scared of losing someone close to me again. If I don't love, then it won't hurt so much when they're gone."

"Fear does not stop death, honey, it stops life. It stops joy. Sure, maybe you spare yourself some pain, but you also prevent yourself from the depth of joy that love brings," she replied.

Miles looked at his mother fully now, face to face, taking in her timeless beauty, the face of home and safety for him. The warmth of her smile, the same crinkling of crow's feet around her eyes that his own face now started to adopt, too. He smiled back at her. A levity rose in him, and he teased, "Mom, when did you get so wise?"

"Like I've said, I've been here all along, just waiting for you to get out of your head and into your heart and talk to me."

"Thank you, mom," Miles said softly. His head was still spinning with the knowledge that his mother was *here* in this garden, available to talk to whenever he wanted, but he wasn't quite ready to wrap his head around being able to talk to her at *any* time. How does one even 'get out of their own head'?

"Louie, no!" Mae's voice came sharp and broke Miles' line of thought. A chubby orange cat was galloping across the yard to the garden toward him with Mae chasing after. "Miles, I am *so* sorry! I was trying to leave you be, but Louie had other ideas." She caught up to him, the cat now lying on his belly, back feet splayed out in back of him, happily munching away on a tomato plant leaf. Mae gathered him up into her arms and he grunted in protest, grasping the leaf of the plant in his mitten-like paw.

Miles couldn't help but laugh at the absurdity of the cat, now pressing his face against Mae's while she held him like a baby. Miles stole a glance beside him, but already knew his mother was no longer there. "It's alright, we had a good talk," he replied, scratching Louie's chin. Once the pond brimmed with water, Miles returned the hose to its place. While Mae returned Louie indoors, Miles installed the pond's filter. Mae joined him again to clean up the yard and put their tools away. The next step was to test the pH of the water, allow it to warm, and then add koi to it. But they would save that for another day.

"This is going to be really awesome," Mae remarked, admiring their work.

"We make a good team," Miles replied.

The two stood in each other's presence admiring the pond, neither knowing what to say to the other. Mae longed for Miles to tell her his thoughts and Miles was milling over what his mother said. They spoke at once.

"If you…" Mae started.

"Have you heard of the annual Cove Carnival?" Miles said at the same time.

"I've seen some fliers up around town but don't know much beyond that."

Miles' face lit up, and instantly, Mae could see Miles as a child. "It's the best weekend of the year! Funnel cakes, rides, games that are likely rigged so you can never win, the whole thing. It's a fundraiser for the city's volunteer fire department. Anyway, it's next weekend and we should go."

"We?" Mae smiled at his amusement.

"Yes, we." Miles bit his bottom lip in anticipation. He gathered her hands between both of his. "Please?"

"Yeah OK, that sounds like a good time." Mae tried to play it cool, not letting the hope of her emotions get the best of her. Miles moved his hands to her waist as hers found their way around his neck and the two embraced.

"I can't wait," he murmured into the top of her head.

✶✶✶✶✶✶

Midweek, Mae sat cross-legged on her porch with her laptop perched in her lap, searching for jobs. What she wanted to do she really had no idea, but what she needed to do was make money. "Thanks, capitalist society," she thought to herself as she scrolled through endless postings that all listed the same vague requirements and job responsibilities. Mae was grateful she lived in a time when a remote job was not difficult to come by but was also resentful that she was from a time where she was taught that a job should also be a passion and vocation. She was resentful for the pressure it put on finding the *right* career, for the pickiness it instilled in her, and for the annoyance she felt at herself for being picky when she was currently unemployed.

She continued scrolling listings pertinent to her last position and read one aloud to herself, "'Are you ready to join a dynamic, fast-paced team?'" she exhaled, "Hmm, do you have something more slow-paced and chill?" Mae never understood the hustle of corporate ladder climbing, but since the layoff, looked at a career as merely a means to support her life outside of it. After sending her resume to four different employers, she closed her laptop and sighed more out of defeat than hopefulness. Louie, lying next to her feet, soaking up the sun, let out a long sigh that mirrored hers.

"I know. It must be really tough for you right now," Mae said mockingly while she massaged the sweet spot behind his ears. "What a rough time you're having as a house kitty of leisure." Mae sat back and sipped her coffee, watching the neighbors in their cars on the way to work. She thought about her neighbor Patty and wondered what she did for work before she retired, then realized she hadn't seen Patty in a few days, which was unusual, given their shared daily habit of porch sitting—both morning and late afternoon. Mae returned her laptop and Louie inside and slipped on a pair of sandals before she walked to Patty's house, her heart beating faster in her chest as she approached. She wasn't sure why she was nervous, but nervous all the same. Was Patty OK?

Mae pushed open the door of the screened-in porch and entered. She was refreshed by the overhead fan blowing a breeze through her hair and stopped for a moment to enjoy it. She extended her hand and pushed the doorbell with her index finger, returning her hand to her pocket. After a minute or so of no answer, she knocked on the door and said, "Patty? It's Mae. Are you there?" She heard a rustle and then footsteps beyond the door.

Patty appeared, pale against the dark room behind her. Her eyes were red and her skin sallow. The corners of her mouth turned up at the sight of Mae, but Mae was not convinced. She gathered Patty into her arms and hugged her tight. "Oh, Patty." She held her for several moments before she asked, "What's going on?" Patty's feeble arms slithered around Mae's waist and hugged her back. The worst part of being a widow was the sudden lack of physical human contact and she intended to soak every bit of it up. Mae stroked her hair, still hugging, and repeated more softly, "What's going on?"

Patty sniffled and managed, "I'm sorry for you to see me like this."

"Nonsense," Mae responded.

Patty took a deep breath in and let it go, stepping back from Mae. "It was the anniversary of Earl's death yesterday, and it's our wedding anniversary today. All the emotions." She gestured expansively to the air in front of her. A tear leaked out from one eye, and Patty brushed it away before it landed.

"Oh Patty, I'm so sorry," Mae lamented, "that's a lot." They both lowered into Patty's porch rocking chairs, Mae never taking her eyes off Patty. Her hair was disheveled and her color pale. She looked tired but alert. Mae couldn't imagine what she must be feeling but knew it was important for her not to shy away.

"It's alright, honey. Most years it goes by with little fanfare and, yes, it's sad, but grief is a sneaky devil. Sometimes it just sneaks up on you and hits you harder than you expected, and well," she gestured at her general appearance, "here we are."

"Can I get you anything?" Mae asked. "Coffee? Tea?"

"A tea would be lovely, dear."

Mae retreated to the house she'd been in just once before, fumbling her way around the kitchen to find Patty's tea and mugs. The teapot, thankfully, was kept charmingly on the stove—its regular post. A tall wooden shelf held numerous tin tea boxes that Patty had collected through the years. Of course, tea was not commonly sold in tins anymore but rather cardboard boxes, so Mae knew these were just for looks. She found the tea bags in a small wooden box in a cupboard over the stove. Once the water heated, she steeped a bag of chamomile, adding just a touch of honey the way Patty preferred, and returned to the porch. Patty gratefully accepted the mug and drank a long sip.

Mae asked, "Do you want to talk? Or do you want to just be?"

"That's a kind offer, Mae. I'm OK though, really. Just had a couple of down days. I'm not sure I'm too up for talking, but I do love you being here," Patty explained.

"Then be here I will," Mae responded, leaning back in the rocking chair. They sat like that for some time—Patty sipping her tea, legs crossed at the ankles, and Mae rocking back and forth watching the cars drive by and the neighbors walk their dogs along the sidewalk that passed through their yards. Suddenly a thought occurred to Mae—the garden. If she could talk to Lucy and Miles could talk to his mother, then maybe…

"Are you up for a walk? Just to my backyard. I want to show you something," Mae asked.

"Oh sure, I don't see why not," Patty obliged. She followed Mae out the porch and down the steps, across the sidewalk and around Mae's bungalow. The garden and pond welcomed them with the sounds of chirping chickadees and butterflies floating from flower to flower. "Oh, honey, you brought back the pond," Patty exclaimed, placing a hand kindly to her heart.

"Brought it back?" Mae asked.

"John, Lucy's dad, had a pond here way back when. It was beautiful and serene and…" she paused, taking stock of the pond in front of her, "remarkably similar to this one. That's incredible."

"How weird is that…?" Mae pondered. "When I dug down for the hole, there was this preexisting liner precisely where I was digging for this pond."

Patty settled onto the cement bench with a smile. Her demeanor instantly changed. Her brow softened, shoulders relaxed, breath evened, and hands folded in her lap. Her eyes followed the fluttering path of a monarch from one milkweed to another. She was at ease. "It sounds like you were called here to do it," she said softly with a glint in her eyes. "Mae, what you told me about Lucy here…do you think?"

"Yes! Of course. That's why I brought you, to give you space. I'll be up on the porch; you just holler if you need anything."

And with that Mae retreated, leaving Patty the space to grieve and talk to Lucy or Earl or whomever she needed. As she exited the garden, she noticed a foil-wrapped candy on the stanchion post, gathered it in her hand, and smiled at the 'wonderful absurdity'—as Patty had put it—at what this garden had become.

18

THE CARNIVAL

Mae, 2022

The week leading up to the summer carnival brought an anxious buzz about the town. The stories of prior years' hurrahs and anticipation of this year's events seemed to be the only topic of conversation. Everyone from the local butcher to kids in the street to bar patrons were excitedly conversing about it. Patty overheard her old schoolmate, Linda, in the grocery store discussing the festival dunk tank. "I hear Fire Chief Sam is even going to participate...that man in a soaked uniform," she fanned herself with her grocery list.

Patty chimed in, "Ooh, Linda don't get my hopes up you little deviant." The women laughed and continued on speculating what the carnival would bring. Mae heard rumors about everything from Bon Jovi as the evening entertainment to a horse and carriage ride around the park. She largely ignored them, not only because her experience of small-town gossip was that it usually was quite an inflation of reality, but also because no amount of gossip could detract from her excitement of experiencing it with Miles. She replayed the way his face lit up and the innocent smile painted across his face when he told her about it. Because it had been so hot outside lately, she had done little gardening, however, no less talking to Lucy. She seemed to show up in Mae's dreams more and more frequently, each dream more lucid and real feeling than the last. Mae was beginning to wonder if she needed the garden at all to see Lucy, but then reminded herself none of this ever happened until she discovered the garden.

 Saturday came and after a leisurely morning of running, enjoying coffee, and job searching on her porch, Mae retreated to the upstairs bathroom to be ready for Miles by mid-afternoon. She dressed in her favorite cutoff jean shorts and a coral-colored tank. It was a sticky, humid, telltale Midwest summer day, so she pulled her hair over one shoulder and braided it, tossing it back over her shoulder when she finished. She applied minimal makeup and just as she was slipping her purse strap over her body, the doorbell rang. Miles awaited, holding a bouquet of pink and yellow dahlias.

 Mae opened the door and gasped, then closed her eyes and inhaled deeply. "How did you know these are my favorite?!"

 Miles smiled proudly. "Lucky guess? Beautiful flowers for a beautiful lady," he said as he held them out for her to take. Mae blushed and stood on her tiptoes to thank him with a kiss on his cheek. She brought the bouquet inside and placed it in a vase of water, to be admired later.

 "You're so sweet," Mae remarked. The two set out toward downtown, walking along the sidewalk of Main Street. Mae loved many things about her new small-town life, but walking everywhere might be her favorite. Sure, she could walk to places in Chicago, but the entire spirit of the place was different—rushed, anonymous. In Cale Cove, everything you needed was just steps away and you were guaranteed to see a friendly, familiar face virtually wherever the day took you; something in which Mae, an extrovert, reveled.

 Miles smoothly slipped Mae's hand in his, lacing their fingers together as they walked, and she looked up at him as he did. His sly smile awaited permission, "Is this OK?" Mae swallowed the butterflies in her chest and nodded yes.

As they approached the downtown "square," the park where they had their picnic was hardly recognizable. Large red and white striped tents, food trucks, a stage with live music, and various carnival rides now sprawled the entire park. The atmosphere was energetic and joyful as screams filled the air of revelers twirling around in rides. The smell of corn dogs, funnel cakes, and onion rings mixed with the sweet wafting scent of cotton candy that blended with kettle corn and fresh taffy hung heavy in the air. Mae's eyes darted from one scene to another, taking it all in. After a minute, she realized Miles was watching her in amusement and she smiled back at him. "Let's do it!" he said.

Moments later, they stood in front of the array of rides with freshly purchased tickets clutched in their hands, assessing which ride was daring enough to be their first. They decided on one that resembled a giant top in which they were strapped to the edges, standing, facing the center. The ride started spinning, and as it did, tilted bit by bit until it appeared the top was on its side. Mae screamed out of excitement and Miles reached his hand over to clasp hers. She watched and he gritted his teeth and closed his eyes, letting out a yell followed by a laugh. "We might be *crazy...*" his words drew out as the ride spun faster. Mae couldn't help but laugh at Miles and by the time the ride slowed and returned to the ground, her stomach and cheeks hurt from laughing so much. Miles' hair was windblown and standing on end and he stumbled as he walked off, helping Mae out of her restraint. They giggled and held each other's arms, stumbling toward a nearby bench.

"Well, that was insane," Mae laughed.

They sat for a bit, calming their spinning senses with corndogs and lemonades. After some time, Miles said, "Hey, I want to apologize to you. I know I got kind of distant after the picnic and it was nothing to do with you. I was..." he hesitated, but seeing Mae's concern and reassuring attentiveness urged him to continue. "I was scared," he finished. Miles was staring at his lap, fidgeting with the hem on his shorts, then met Mae's eyes. She looked concerned and sad and confused all at the same time.

"I don't understand. Scared?"

Miles exhaled. "Scared of getting hurt. I really like you, Mae, and the more I allow that feeling to grow, the bigger the risk of getting hurt. But someone made me realize that stifling that chance of getting hurt also cuts off the depth of the wonderful feeling of…well, this," he said, gesturing between the two of them. "Anyway, I hope you'll forgive me, and also that we're on the same page because that would be pretty awkward if not."

Mae laughed. "Of course I forgive you. I get it. Relationships are scary and risky, and you never really know what you're going to get when you wear your heart on your sleeve, but" she took his hand in her own, "I'd love to find out with you." Mae watched as Miles moved closer to her and cupped her face in his hand, gently kissing her and lingering on her lips for a moment.

"Well, isn't this the sweetest thing I *never* saw coming," came a cheery, sarcastic voice beside them. They pulled apart to see who was watching them.

"Patty!" Mae impulsively touched her fingertips to her lips, maybe to seal in the kiss or to cover her tracks in bashfulness. Patty laughed and gave them a small wave with the hand that had a bag of kettle corn wrapped around it.

"Now you know I'm giving you a hard time!" Patty seemed to be enjoying herself and Mae and Miles laughed along with her. Patty said to Miles, "I'm glad your mother talked some sense into you. See you kids later," she winked and walked off into the carnival.

"Your mom…in the garden?" Mae asked.

"Yep," Miles bowed his head bashfully.

"I'm so glad," Mae replied.

"You're really something special, rehabbing that garden and sharing it with me and Patty. It's really generous of you," Miles said.

Mae bowed her head graciously and they shared a few comfortable moments of silence, sitting on the bench.

Then, Mae raised an eyebrow playfully and suggested, "What do you say we joust?"

"Joust...Mae?" But she was already off to an enormous inflatable wrestling ring with what appeared to be a balance beam stretched across it. Two people stood atop it with puffy cushioned helmets on, grasping what appeared to be a giant puffy Q-tip. Miles quickly followed after Mae and joined her at the side of the jousting ring as the two inside slapped each other with their jousting sticks, laughing hysterically, until one fell off the beam and a horn sounded, indicating the end of the match. There was no line, so Miles and Mae approached the entrance and timidly donned the helmets and shirked their shoes.

Mae entered the ring first, skipping across the beam to the other side with the jousting stick above her head as if she were a WWE champion with their belt held high in celebration. Miles laughed and said, "I wouldn't get too cocky if I were you. I have impeccable balance. The only one falling off this beam is you." Mae chuckled in return.

"If you say so, coffee man! A little trash talk doesn't scare me!"

A gentleman in a black and white striped shirt wearing a whistle around his neck entered the ring and stepped between Mae and Miles, one at each end of the beam. "Alright kids, I want a clean match! Well, really anything goes and you're not going to hurt yourself in this inflatable cloud, so have at it! Last man...ahem...or woman standing wins!" With a sharp blow of his whistle, the referee jumped off the beam and backed away, hanging out at the edge of the ring to supervise. Mae and Miles now faced each other, grinning beneath their cushioned helmets.

Mae waited only a second before she lunged forward, swinging her doubled-ended puff stick in a chopping motion, the log she aimed to split being Miles' body. He raised his stick just in time to block hers from knocking into his shoulder, but he still stumbled off balance. He stumbled a few steps and regained his composure while Mae squealed in excitement. Miles shrugged his shoulders and rolled his head from side to side, "Oh, now we're warming up I see, alright." He whipped his jousting stick low, going for Mae's ankles. She jumped to avoid it, but the toes of one foot caught and she fell onto the beam. Lying on her stomach, straddling the beam she exhaled sharply, blowing a rogue strand of hair from her face. Miles regained his stance as Mae pushed herself back up to standing. "Well damn," she said playfully.

A crowd was beginning to gather around the ring and after they exchanged several more swipes unsuccessfully dismounting the other, Mae heard her name from the crowd. "Yeaaah Mae, baby, knock him over, you got this!" Her eyes broke away from Miles for a second to see just beyond him at a red-faced, wild-haired Cassie cheering her on.

"Hey, we were friends first! The betrayal!" Miles directed at Cassie.

"Sorry, Mileman, she's my girl now," Cassie shrugged.

Mae seized the opportunity of a split-second distraction in Miles' line of vision to first swipe right, then flip her stick around to swing left, surprising him. The puffy end of the jousting stick contacted his middle, and he immediately swayed like he was keeping an invisible hula hoop airborne. "Gah!" he yelled, unable to regain his footing and tumbling onto the inflatable mat below. The referee stepped out onto the playing area again and chimed his air horn.

"Ladies and gentlemen, we have a champion!" Mae dropped her stick as the referee grabbed her hand and hoisted it in the air in celebration. Cassie whistled loudly, two fingers stuck in her mouth and others clapped at Miles' defeat. Mae strode over to him, still lying on the mat, and extended her hand to help him up.

"Good match, my friendly foe," she offered.

Miles grabbed her hand but instead of using it for leverage to stand, yanked and pulled her over onto the mat beside him. He pulled off her helmet, brushed the stray hair off her face, and kissed her with both hands around her face. "Good match."

"Ow *owww*!" Mae heard Cassie yell in the background. They both got up, and after returning their jousting materials and thanking the referee, joined Cassie outside the ring, but not before Mae snuck in a smug bow to her onlookers.

"You guys were fantastic!" Cassie exclaimed. A dark-haired woman who Mae had not seen before was standing next to Cassie—Smitha—Mae guessed, and confirmed when Cassie said, "Oh my gosh, Mae! This is my girlfriend Smitha I've told you about." Smitha extended her arms for a greeting hug, and Mae leaned into it.

"It's so nice to finally meet you! Are you up next?" Mae asked. Smitha nervously nodded while Cassie bounced in excitement. Miles and Mae watched them enter the ring, donning the same goofy puffed helmets and double-sided jousting sticks they did, walking the balance beam to the center of the ring. The referee gave them even less instruction than he did Miles and Mae and instead blew his whistle and backed away quickly. Miles and Mae watched with other onlookers what turned out to be a rather short match between Smitha and Cassie in which Smitha beat Cassie with one swing and Cassie could barely get up, she was laughing so hard. After regaining their composure and passing the jousting sticks to the next in line, the four of them set out for the carnival games.

Cassie proved to be a natural talent at popping balloons with darts, and Miles didn't miss knocking over a single glass milk bottle he targeted with a baseball. When Mae looked surprised, he shrugged and said, "I played baseball in college." While Smitha and Mae turned up empty handed on games, Miles and Cassie won inflatable swords, which they proceeded to fight each other with while Mae and Smitha watched giggling. "I'm so glad I got to see Cassie as a ten-year-old today," said Smitha, very amused. "She's so serious at work; I had no idea that all this time, she had a competitive steak hiding deep down." While Cassie and Miles continued to lunge at each other, the foursome moved toward the funhouse at the end of the alley of games.

Cassie and Smitha went first, followed by Mae and Miles. They worked their way first over a very wobbly bridge, which brought them to a rotating tunnel that reminded Mae of television shows' depiction of a time warp. Miles sprinted through, barely stumbling, and Mae followed suit. They high fived and moved onto a mirror maze, where they barreled into no less than three mirrors before they found their way through. The funhouse ended with a swirled tube slide. Miles slid down first and when Mae met him at the bottom, he was crouched at the foot of the slide such that her coming out of the slide landed her on his back. He grabbed her legs and stood, sweeping Mae into a piggyback, while she laughed all the way. She couldn't believe how much fun she was having and how natural it felt to be with Miles. She couldn't believe it had taken them this long.

Cassie and Smitha had set off toward the bandshell and Miles followed in close pursuit with Mae on his back, yelling, "Mush! Mush!" An 80s cover band was playing, and they were shockingly good. People from Patty's age down to children gathered to listen, jumping and dancing to their classic rock covers. Mae slid off Miles' back and planted her feet on the ground again, glad to be here with her new friends. They stood for several minutes, swaying to the music, when she felt a pull on her left hand. Miles was to her right, so she startled and looked toward who touched her.

"I've missed you," said a menacing voice. Mae had blissfully not heard his voice in a while, but it was unmistakable.

"Jared," she said accusingly.

He laughed with his head tilted back and his eyelids lazy, smelling of booze. "Is that all the warm welcome I get?

Come here." Jared tried to pull Mae to him in a hug, but Mae pulled back hard, bumping into Miles.

"Mae, who is this guy? Is he bothering you?" Miles asked.

"Who the hellareyou?" Jared said, slurring his words together. "Mae's my girlfriend. Always 'as been. Guessing she didn't tell you."

Miles stepped between them and placed a hand on Jared's chest to put distance between him and Mae. "Miles, don't," Mae said. "It's not worth it. Jared, you need to leave. I mean it. You shouldn't be here."

"Ooh is this your bodyguard? What do you think I'm gonna do, bodyguard?" Jared taunted. Miles was at least five inches taller than Jared but that didn't deter him. He pushed Miles' hand away and grabbed Mae again, roughly. He grasped both of her shoulders in his hands and aggressively kissed her before she pushed him away, slapping his cheek.

"Jared, what the hell?" Mae spotted a police officer walking through the crowd toward them, watching the commotion.

"You need to leave Mae alone. Get out of here," Miles said calmly. Hearing Mae's name come from Miles' mouth enraged Jared further, and he swung a fist around to meet Miles' face, but Miles' reflexes were quicker. He stepped back, leaving Jared's momentum to toss him forward onto the dusty ground below.

Mae helped him up and led him aside, trying to talk some sense into him. She caught Miles' eye and couldn't quite read his expression—a mix of confusion, impatience, and anger. She sat Jared on a bench nearby and went back to Miles. "Let me talk to him and see if I can get him out of here," she said. Miles nodded curtly and glared at Jared as she returned to him. The rest of the day didn't go as Mae had hoped. Mae tried to understand why Jared was in Cale Cove and how he even knew where to find her, but he was making less and less sense the more he talked. The most she got out of him was he was still in love with her and believed she was "going through a phase" he declared over. Mae was fed up and offered to call him a rideshare from his phone. He said he didn't have anywhere to go; he had driven to Cale Cove on a whim (is that how all outsiders get here?) and there were no hotels in Cale Cove.

She couldn't let him drive home in his intoxicated state, so begrudgingly, Mae walked him back to her bungalow, showing him the couch and tossing him a blanket. Moments later, he was fast asleep, and she was wondering what she would say to Miles. As she watched her ex-boyfriend lying on her couch, mouth ajar and a slumbering cacophony escaping him, Mae realized she no longer wished him any harm, but she sure as hell didn't wish to spend another minute with him.

"Ugh, what a mess," she lamented to herself. She walked herself up to bed, locking the bedroom door behind her. Tomorrow she would make this up to Miles.

19

APOLOGIES

Lucy, 1994

"Right this way, Ms. Brown," said an older, heavyset woman in a knit cardigan, carrying a manila folder of papers. She gestured down a short hallway behind a reception desk.

Two of the office walls were covered in mahogany bookshelves, the third with historic exposed brick, and the fourth with floor-to-ceiling windows and views of the bustling downtown outside. Well, bustling in the way that small towns bustled with mothers tending to young ones in strollers, business owners sweeping off their front stoops, delivery trucks stopping to stock the florist, deli, and cafe with the day's provisions. Inside, there was an air of stale papers and oolong tea, with a touch of vanilla. A corner fireplace and the stiff office armchairs facing it softened the professionally austere decor with a touch of comfort. A middle-aged woman perched on the edge of one chair rose from her seat, collecting her purse. "Oh please, dear, call me Lucy."

The cardigan woman walked slowly in her low, sensible heels, leading Lucy down the hallway, stopping in front of a glass-walled conference room where a man wearing a well-fitted suit awaited. She pushed open the door of the room to let Lucy inside, and the man stood, smoothing his jacket. He extended a hand in greeting, "Ms. Brown, it's a pleasure to meet you. I'm Michael Robertson, the attorney handling your mother's will. My deepest condolences for the circumstances that bring you here, but it is a pleasure to meet you." The man was young, Lucy guessed perhaps in his 30s, and tall. His dark hair was parted on the side and combed so slick not a single hair was out of place. His eyes held a warm sincerity she wasn't expecting from an attorney.

"Oh, thank you," Lucy accepted his hand between the both of hers and lowered her eyes. "Thank you for your condolences, mister…uh…Robertson."

"Please. Call me Michael."

"Michael. I'm not sure what exactly to expect here. I just got a letter and…" Lucy trailed off.

"Not to worry! Take a seat and I'll explain everything. Can I get you anything to make you more comfortable? Perhaps have Donna make you a tea?"

"No, thank you," Lucy declined gratefully. "I'm quite alright." She took a deep breath in and exhaled slowly. "I had no idea that my mother…" Lucy took another deep breath. "I had no idea that she even had a will. This is all taking me a bit off guard."

"I understand that this can all be a little overwhelming," Michael gestured to the stack of papers in front of him, then folded his hands over them. "My job is to assist the executor of the estate to carry out your mother's wishes."

"And the named executor…?" Lucy asked.

"Is you," Michael confirmed.

Lucy's eyebrows lifted high, and her mouth opened to say something, then closed.

"I take it you're surprised by this news," Michael conjectured.

Lucy closed her eyes and nodded. "My mother and I," she swallowed, "weren't close."

"Well, we'll get to the nitty gritty of it all, but I want you to know that when your mother made this will with me, she was very adamant that you receive the entirety of her estate, most notably the property at," Michael checked his notes, "444 Main St. here in town."

"She wanted *me* to have the house. Are you sure?" Lucy racked her brain for the last time she and her mother had spoken, coming up empty.

"I'm quite sure, Ms. Brown. And while it's not typical, she did leave me a letter to ensure you read upon this occasion." Michael reached into the manila folder and pulled out an envelope. Her mother's neat cursive on the front spelled *Lucinda Antoinette*. Lucy's bewilderment in accepting the envelope from Michael prompted him to say, "I'll give you a few moments alone." He stepped out of the room, softly closing the door.

Lucy inhaled and exhaled a few deep breaths before breaking the envelope's seal. She delicately pulled out the folder paper inside and began to read.

My dearest Lucinda,

If you're reading this, my time has come, and the Lord has called me home. I have asked Michael to hold this letter for me for this occasion because there is something I needed to tell you that I've never quite been able to put aside my pride to say in life. I have always regretted the deterioration of our relationship. Your father's death was hard on all of us, but hindsight has had me reflect in a way to see it through the eyes of a seventeen-year-old girl whose best friend was her father. I cannot imagine the pain you were going through and the hardship I added on with the expectations I laid on you after.

Part of me thinks I did so because you reminded me so much of me, and I felt that if I could handle this then you should, too. But you were a girl. I pushed you away because my heart did not know how to heal nor that the healing included sharing with you. I hope that one day you will be able to forgive me for the way that things transpired, for the way that once you left town after the wedding, I felt relief.

There is no one more deserving of our home than you, Antoinette. If you choose to sell it and split the proceeds with your siblings, that is your decision, but the house, the garden, everything is yours. I hope you will accept this as a token of my regrets in life and think less harshly of me in reflection.

I love you always,

Lucinda Rose (your mother)

Lucy held the letter loosely as if it might burst into flame at any moment. She read it and re-read it. Her head was a swirl of memories and regrets, wondering how things might have been different if her mother had said these words to her sooner. A tear streaked down one cheek, then the other. She swiftly wiped them away and told herself, "No point. No point in wondering what is no longer possible." A soft knock on the glass door drew Lucy's eyes to the room's entry.

Michael cracked the door open, pushing only his face over the threshold, despite the fact that Lucy could see his whole body through the glass. "May I return?"

"Yes, of course," Lucy said, waving him in. "Thank you for that time."

"Are you ready to begin going through how this will work?" Michael asked carefully.

Lucy wiped her eyes one more time and sat up straight. "Yes," she smiled. "Let's do it."

20

AFTERMATH

Mae, 2022

Mae awoke to the doorbell ringing followed by a soft knock at the door. She pulled on shorts and a sweatshirt over her sleep shirt and padded her way down the stairs just as Jared (*crap*—he was still here) was opening the door, wearing only his boxers and very chiseled physique. "Jared—don't—I've got it," she said hurriedly, wishing he would just go away.

A deep and familiar voice sounded from behind the door, "You again. I'm looking for Mae."

Mae's stomach sunk. Jared pushed the door all the way open to reveal Miles standing there, his sweet self looking handsome as ever in a pressed linen shirt and carrying two coffees whose aroma now wafted to her nostrils. Her stomach sank at the sight of him next to a disheveled Jared, now leaning on the door frame, one leg crossed over the other with a smug glare across his face.

Mae pushed Jared away from the door and said, "Miles, I can explain…"

Miles noted in her appearance and then looked back at Jared, the two of them both obviously having just woken up. He pushed the coffees into Mae's hands and stepped back.

"Don't bother. I came here thinking I needed to apologize for being childish when you left last night, but now…I don't really have words anymore." Miles stepped down the porch and out to the sidewalk faster than Mae could form a sentence.

"Miles, wait!" she shouted after him, jogging to keep up.

"Don't," he said as he kept walking. Mae was suddenly aware of the fact that cars driving by were watching. She blew a strand of hair from her forehead in a sharp exhale and stopped, crossing her arms over her chest.

"Miles," she yelled after him. "I'll call you later." Miles kept walking but raised a hand in acknowledgement.

Mae returned to the house where Jared was drinking one of the coffees Miles brought. "This is good coffee," he said nonchalantly.

"You need to leave," she said to him. She picked up his discarded clothes from the arm of the couch, threw them at his chest, and collected his shoes from the door, also shoving them in his chest.

"What, is that your boyfriend?" Jared snickered. "Come on, Mae, cut this little rebellion out. You know you belong in Chicago with me. This has been cute but it's time to come back home."

"THIS is my home now, Jared. You had no right to intrude. We are DONE here. We're done. We've been done. I do not want this anymore. I don't know how many different ways I can say it to get through to you." For a moment, Mae thought he might try to refute it again, but then something miraculous happened. He set down the coffee that wasn't his, slipped on his shoes, and straightened up.

"If this is what you really want, then I'll go." he said. "But don't come groveling back to me when you realize what you've lost. I'm the best you can do," he paused to caress her cheek with a finger. "You'll figure it out soon enough. Jared out." He slammed the front door behind him and walked briskly to his car waiting at the curb outside. Mae exhaled in relief as she watched him go, then laughed as he picked a parking ticket off of his windshield before getting in the car and driving away.

"Thank God that's over," she said to herself.

When emotions ran high and she didn't know how to deal, Mae always went for a run. She drank the coffee Miles brought her—with a sprinkle of cinnamon and nutmeg in it, like he knew she liked it—and changed into running clothes. Some days running feels easy and effortless, like you're gliding across the pavement and all of nature smiles down on you. Then some days every step feels like an effort and you're wondering why you bothered. This day was the latter. Mae alternated walking and running until she reached a bench along the lake path and collapsed into a seat. She picked up a rock at her feet and threw it into the water; it landed with a loud and splashy clunk.

It was so like Jared to drop in at the most inopportune time after hearing nothing from him for months. She couldn't believe his ego, acting like he owned her or like she owed him something. If there was anything Mae had learned from her time in Cale Cove, it was that she would rather be single forever than to believe once again that she needed someone like Jared to feel worthy of love. Lucy had helped her realize that. She's always been a creative and unique soul capable of putting love into the world independent of a boyfriend, as evidenced by the warmth of everyone she'd met in Cale Cove. They were drawn to her light. Why had she thought she needed a significant other to feel whole? Being around Jared again flooded her with the feelings of inadequacy that he always inspired in her—that she needed him to somehow feel validated. No more. Mae validated herself.

She picked up another stone and threw it, hard. The guttural screech of a sandhill crane startled her and her foot nearly slipped into the water. She looked at the crane watching her. "What? What are you gonna do? I've had a rough last 24 hours, OK?" The bird flapped its wings and turned its back to her, uninterested in the drama of her love life.

Later that day, Mae decided to go to The Crooked Cask for dinner. Nothing sounded better to her than a Reuben melt and sweet potato fries. When she entered the bar, it was largely empty, save for Cassie behind it and a middle-aged man at the far side of the bar, drinking a beer and scrolling through his phone. She hoisted herself into a seat on a barstool on the other end and greeted Cassie, "Hey you."

"Hey…" Cassie said expectantly. "What's goin on?" She poured Mae's favorite and Mae gratefully accepted, taking a long sip before delving into how the last 24 hours transpired. Cassie's expression went from curious to surprised to indignant. Mae had previously told her briefly of her relationship with Jared but didn't go too far into detail as to the kind of person he turned out to be. With his showing up at the carnival, Cassie didn't need to imagine to fill in the details. Cassie's mouth hung open and her brow furrowed while Mae finished the story and took another sip of her hazy IPA.

"And he just *expected* that you would take him back just like that no questions asked? What an…" Cassie ranted.

"Idiot," Mae interjected. "I know." She sighed deeply. "What am I going to tell Miles? He was so sweet coming over with coffee this morning just for it all to be thrown back in his face," she paused remembering Jared's state of undress as he answered the door. "Ugh, Cassie. It looked really bad. I really didn't mean for things to happen like this."

"Of course you didn't," Cassie covered Mae's hand with her own. "Just give him time to cool off and then you can explain things. Miles is an understanding guy and I know he's really into you." Cassie turned her back to the bar to refill the other patron's mug, but continued talking to Mae, "Not to worry, friend, it'll all work itself out." Mae ate dinner and got the low-down on the rest of the night at the carnival from Cassie. Apparently, Patty and Jim made a great dancing duo when the cover band took a break and Frank Sinatra played through the sound system.

"You wouldn't believe the moves they had!" Cassie went on, "I've known these two my whole life and had no idea. They were laughing and spinning each other around. Jim did that swing move where he, like…tossed her over his back," Cassie tried to imitate it with an imaginary partner behind the bar, making Mae laugh.

"Wow, so random," Mae enjoyed the recounting.

"Seriously. A man of many talents," Cassie replied, then looked to the door as it swung open. "Well, speak of the devil." Jim squinted as he looked around the bar, giving time for his eyes to adjust from the sunlight outside.

"Hello! Who's the devil?"

"You are! I was just telling Mae about your crazy dance moves last night," Cassie replied.

"Dance moves? Me?" Jim pondered this thought for several moments, looking to the ceiling for a clue, then a smile broke over his face. "Yeah, that was me."

"We had no idea you liked to dance, Jim," Mae said.

"I didn't either!" he laughed.

Mae's attention was drawn to the army green cargo vest he was wearing. Three of the four pockets appeared to be filled with something lumpy, and the top right one had the unmistakable yellow, rubbery shape of a limp balloon poking out. "What's with the balloons, Jim?" she asked.

"Balloons?" He again looked confused, then the wave of realization hit. "Oh, balloons!" He plucked the deflated balloon from his pocket and started stretching it mindlessly. "I was making balloon animals in the park. The kids love 'em."

Cassie's attention was piqued, and she asked, "Can you show us how it's done?"

Jim pulled a handheld pump from another vest pocket, attached the balloon's end, and holding it in place on the nozzle, started pumping the balloon full of air. Once satisfied, he pulled it off and tied the end. His hands worked up and down the balloon until he found the correct position and started twisting. Cassie and Mae were held captive watching. "The thing is," he said, "I don't really know how it's done. It just gets done." He shrugged.

"It looks like you know what you're doing to me," Mae said as the head and front legs of a dog appeared between his quick fingers manipulating the balloon this way and that. Another moment later Jim finished the dog, placed it on the bar, and threw his hands up like he had just finished a magic trick.

"Tah dah!" he said. Cassie and Mae applauded him and the man across the bar joined in, having since abandoned whatever was previously holding his attention. "Aw shucks, you guys, thanks," Jim blushed in humility. "It's a weird thing. If I had to explain how to do it, I really don't remember, like most things, but my hands seem to know what to do when they touch the balloon. I remember, but I don't."

"It's just ingrained in you," Cassie offered softly, still fixated on the balloon dog.

Jim shrugged again. "I suppose you're always drawn back to where or what you belong to, you know?"

"Very true, Jim," Mae agreed.

After another round and three more balloon creations, Mae left Cassie and Jim to walk home. She felt her heart swell and fill with love for these people who now felt like family, just strangers a few short months ago. What an unexpected and wonderful summer it had been: finding the town on a whim, having previously thought it to have been a work of fiction from her dear grandmother, then discovering it as a very real and very charming small town a short drive from her hometown. It still didn't make sense to her why she didn't know that Lucy had grown up here, or for that matter, why her entire family believed she had grown up where they had. She had an entire adolescence here and nobody knew. Was Mae drawn back to where she belonged, like Jim suggested?

※※※※※※

  The next morning, Mae dressed and walked to Cove Coffee for her favorite bagel sandwich and coffee. She thought about calling Miles, then decided a face-to-face interaction would be better. As she pushed open the door and its hanging bell chimed to announce her arrival, Miles' voice greeted her with his standard, "Good morning! Welcome to Cove Coffee," but she realized it was an absent-minded, standard greeting he would give to anyone. He didn't look at her from his place at the register because he was deep in conversation with a man on the other side of the counter. The man was wearing a suit and carrying a briefcase in one hand and a stack of papers in the other. His hair was thinning, and Mae guessed him to be in his 60s, but he looked unmistakably like Miles in the future. She caught the end of their conversation.

  "Yeah, I know. I've been waiting for a good time. I guess there is no good time — now is as good of a time as any," Miles said.

  "I agree. I'll get it all together and then you can decide if you want to or should I…?" he trailed off, noticing Mae approaching the register.

  "I'll let you know, thank you," Miles replied, ending the conversation.

  "Thanks, kid, see you for dinner tomorrow," and with a wave to Miles and a nod to Mae, the man left.

  Miles turned his attention to Mae and said, "My father."

  "Oh nice. I didn't realize he was around here."

  "What can I get you?" Miles asked professionally.

  Mae was taken aback by his coldness; Miles knew what she wanted because she was a creature of habit and always ordered the same. "Uh, my usual," she said.

  Miles punched in her order to the tablet and said, "I'll have it out shortly."

The cafe quickly filled with the usual breakfast crowd and Miles, moving swiftly between the register, coffee machine, and kitchen, paid her no mind. Feeling defeated and like she'd need to do something more than show up at his place of business to make things right with him, she regretfully decided to take her breakfast to go.

21

WHERE THERE'S A WILL THERE'S A WAY

Lucy, 1994

A few months had passed since the initial meeting in the attorney's office, and Lucy was now the owner of her childhood home, though she did not live in it. She and Kurt had made their life in Birchfield, where they raised their children. While they were now divorced, they remained friends and both active in the community there. Cale Cove held too many memories for Lucy to want to uproot her life at this point and relive the emotionally difficult times that transpired there. She did consider it, of course, when she initially discovered that her mother had left her the home. She remembered the radiance and beauty the garden held and the peace that filled her when she was in it. But after cleaning out the house of her mother's belongings (keeping some and donating the rest), she decided it was time for a new family to love the house.

Yet she couldn't bring herself to sell it. She'd spoken to a realtor in town, cleaned and prepared everything for showings, and at the last minute got cold feet. It neither felt right to live there nor to sell it. The house was a piece of her, her connection to her roots. She couldn't bear to part with that, no matter how much sadness occurred within its walls.

There was also the layer of guilt that her grown children had no idea she was even here. That she had ever been here. After the grief and impulsivity that led Lucy to leave Cale Cove, she carried shame and regret that morphed into the hands that crafted her new life with Kurt in Birchfield. She never intended to lie to her children, but rather, it became a convenient omission. It was easy when they were young. Kids are too self-absorbed to care about too many details of their parents' lives before they were parents. But now that they were older, she found herself keeping this secret inheritance from them. What was the point of telling them now? A little white lie never hurt anyone.

Lucy hemmed and hawed for weeks about what to do, then finally settled into the decision that felt the most right. She would rent the house. Yes, that seemed like a good solution. It was still hers and there if she ever changed her mind, but she would rent it to someone else. Surely, a family could use the spacious house and vast yard to raise their own family. She'd find someone to act as a landlord in the area, attending to the home's repairs and necessary upkeep, but one more pressing issue occupied Lucy's thoughts regarding the home.

Since working with Michael on carrying out her mother's final wishes, Lucy was considering if she should have a will. She and Kurt never had one of their own together, but now seemed like a pertinent time to consider what she wanted to happen to her estate, especially and notably now, with the Cale Cove Main St. home. This is what brought her back to the office of Michael Robertson, attorney at law, the following week. Donna welcomed her and prepared a mug of peppermint tea while she waited for Michael.

Lucy sipped the tea, taking it in with all of her senses. Her eyes closed and she inhaled the aroma, letting it connect her to memories of the garden. She'd grown peppermint in it that she dried to make into a loose-leaf tea. The scent reminded her of the hours she'd spend alone and with her dad in the garden after he had passed. For a brief moment she wondered if she was making a mistake renting the house.

She'd heard horror stories of people who rented their property to people who didn't care for it as much as they did and disrespected it with carelessness. Her attention was suddenly alerted to the sound of tiny footsteps pattering down the hallway.

"Bye dad!" yelled a little boy with a bowl cut no more than four years old. He ran toward the door, a young woman trailing him. Michael gave her hand a squeeze and kissed her cheek before she and the boy left. Lucy smiled at the joy in the little one.

"You can come on back, Lucy," Michael said, smiling.

"Is that your little one?" Lucy asked as she rose from the chair and followed Michael down the hall.

"Yes, that's my boy Miles and my wife. They bring me lunch on Fridays as a way to kick off the weekend."

"Well, that's lovely," Lucy mused.

The pair entered the conference room and settled in. Michael reviewed the process he typically followed with clients wishing to draft a will. Lucy opened her notebook in which she outlined each of the things she wished to cover in the will. Her children would receive the condo she currently lived in, along with most of her monetary assets. The Cale Cove house was outlined in a separate provision, bequeathed not to her children, but to the next generation she hoped would find their way back to Lucy's roots. Sensitive to parental pressure in decision making though, Lucy was careful to outline precisely how this would be done. Michael advised her it was not typical, to which Lucy laughed and replied, "I am not typical."

Over the next half hour, they hashed out the specifics of the will while Michael scribbled copious notes. He looked them over and asked, "I think there's just one more question that I have for you. Have you considered who you wanted to name as the executor?"

Lucy's mind went to the letter her mother had left with Michael that he gave her upon their first meeting. She was reminded of the first person she ever trusted wholly, the one person in the world who knew her completely. She thought of the regrets she held in her heart, just as her mother had in her own. Lucy removed an envelope from her purse and slid it across the table to Michael. "I believe you're familiar with this concept now," she said with a smirk.

Once the business talk was done, they chatted about Michael's family. Lucy was curious how long they'd been in Cale Cove and if little Miles enjoyed it. Michael told her about how they landed here after he finished law school and found his first job in the closest big city. After getting several years of experience to build his confidence, he decided to open his own practice. The market was already saturated in the city, so they found Cale Cove and thought it was the perfect place to raise Miles and the hope of future children.

"And it is! It's charming and a very close-knit community," Michael said. "Once we find a house that's a bit bigger, we'll really settle in."

"Oh?" Lucy pried.

"Well," Michael said with a giddy grin he could hardly hope to hide, "we just found out that we're expecting another little one at the end of the year."

"Oh, congratulations, Michael! How wonderful for you," Lucy was genuinely happy for him. She had grown quite fond of the young lawyer and wanted good news for him, remembering how much she loved living here as a child, riding bikes through downtown and fishing in the lake. "You need a home, you say?"

"We've been in a two-bedroom apartment since we moved here, wanting to make sure it stuck before we bought a home. When the baby comes, we'll be a bit too tight of a squeeze in that apartment I'm afraid."

"Michael, humor me for a moment. Do you remember why we know each other, the Main St. house?"

Lucy proposed renting the home to Michael and his family. She explained how she loved it, but she was settled elsewhere. The house held many memories that she simultaneously could not let go of yet wanted to distance herself from. At first, he was hesitant, keen on buying over renting, but Lucy assured him they could stay as long as they pleased. "There's really only one stipulation," Lucy warned. "Could you return that garden to its former glory? It really was such a magnificent oasis at one time."

Michael laughed and replied, "Oh, I don't think that will be a problem. My wife has quite the green thumb." He agreed to consider the offer and let Lucy know soon.

Lucy returned to her life in Birchfield. No one back home knew she was ever in Cale Cove.

22

LOUIE'S JAUNT

Louie, 2022

The move to Cale Cove has been glorious. My human previously stuffed me into a tiny apartment with the most repugnant dog smells wafting up the fire escape. There were lots of sounds—too many—coming from outside. Sirens. All the time. Day and night there were sirens. People talking, singing, yelling. It was like no one respected my quiet time. I am a descendent of the king of the jungle but they paid no mind. I need at least sixteen hours of beauty rest per day because I need to watch over my human at night. Did you know humans close their eyes for EIGHT hours a day? How is a cat supposed to know she's not dead? Anyway, the house we're in now is very much an upgrade. Mae lets me have free reign of the house all day and sometimes I even get to go outside. OK, maybe I let myself out for a bit before she races after me to come back in. I don't know why she's so concerned with me going on outdoor adventures. I am an apex predator after all. I've killed at least three mice in the basement.

Anyway, there was a day last week that Mae went for a run in the morning, and I slipped my svelte body through the screen door before it slammed shut. My stealth rendered her oblivious to the escape and I earned myself some fine time in the sunshine without anyone reminding me I don't have any front claws. I did a lap around the yard to make sure all was in order, then sprawled out on the front lawn. It was already warm with the morning sun and resting my belly upon it with the sun warming my back felt as close to heaven as I can imagine. I ate some grass, and it honestly didn't taste good, but it's something I don't get to do inside so it was a compulsion I had to obey. I might have fallen asleep for a bit, but I don't think so. Remember? Apex predator.

    Suddenly there was a small human running toward me. Now, I'm a pretty reasonable cat, but small humans are just not something I do. Why are they so loud? Why are their movements so sudden? Always trying to smash my ears or pull my tail. If only they knew what I am capable of. Regular humans are just alright, so tiny ones are intolerable. I was relieved when I realized the goblin boy was not in fact running toward me, but rather after a shiny object. Glittering and spinning in the sunlight, it enraptured me. I don't want to be in competition with the goblin boy, but I found myself unable to tear my eyes away from the small, erratic object.

    Mae and I watched *Harry Potter* once and I think this is how he felt about catching the golden snitch. This is never something I envisioned myself wanting, but now that it is in front of me, absolutely nothing in the world will stop me from making it mine. So, I used my unmatched prowess to leap from the long grass and swipe the shining orb. In one effortless swoop of my paw, I had it in my mouth.

    "Hey! That's mine! That's my bouncy ball!"

    Shit. The goblin boy was following me, arms outstretched in desperation. I had no choice but to run, but the weight of my masculinity—Mae calls it a pooch—swaying under me slowed me to a pace the goblin boy was able to match. We both ran to the backyard, and I sought refuge in the garden beneath the mulberry tree. I was more interested in the goblin boy not chasing me than I was at the ball at this point, so I dropped it in the bed of coneflowers and rested by the pond.

Not a moment later, the boy was in the garden with me, wiping off his ball on his shirt. "Thanks, cat." He leaned down and petted not the normal place between my ears, but rather, scratched under my chin. The goblin boy became less of a goblin by knowing the secret scratch spot, so I allowed him to continue. It was so relaxing that I couldn't help but purr. Surely, he understood this was a one-time enjoyment and expected no future affection from me. I rolled onto my back to seek more scratches when he sat down in the garden next to me.

"Hey, you kinda remind me of my dog."

What an absolutely preposterous thing to say, Goblin.

"His name was Hank. He died last year."

That's actually heartbreaking. I feel for the kid. Dogs really love humans and from the distant sadness in the boy's eyes, I can assume he cared for Hank a lot, too. My better judgment aside, I climbed into the boy's lap to give him a tail hug. You know, just caressing my tail to his face so I don't have to commit to a full body hug. Those are far too problematic.

"Thanks, kitty. You're a nice cat." He proceeded to pet me, so I curled up on his lap, hoping to comfort him just a bit.

"Hank was a golden retriever. That's why you remind me of him. You're both orange and really soft," he explained while tracing my stripes with his stubby little fingers. We sat like that for a while. My eyes closed with the slow realization this goblin wasn't going to pull my tail. He was gentle and Hank must have been a lucky dog to have been loved by one of the few good tiny humans.

Suddenly, I heard the unmistakable jingle of a dog's collar tag shaking. The boy exclaimed, "Hank!" but I knew he must be mistaken. He just told me Hank died last year. I let one eye open slowly, waiting for this delusion to be over so he could get back to petting me when I saw, without a doubt, a golden retriever standing before us in the garden. I could not wrap my mind around what was happening. The boy's hands left me, and both drew up to cover his heart. In exasperation he said, "Hank! I've missed you so much, buddy!"

Hang hopped up and down, tail wagging with impossible speed side to side. He was just as happy to see the goblin boy as he was to see him. Hank's mouth was ajar, his parted lips peeled back over his teeth revealing the biggest dog smile I have ever seen. Typically, when I am this close to a dog, I begin reciting my final words, but this dog meant no harm. In fact, his eyes were unmistakably filled with the most love I have ever seen carried by an animal before. As the boy rose to go greet the dog, I slid off his lap as my attention was drawn elsewhere.

"Louie? Louie?" It was Mae back from her run. Uh oh. I should have been back inside by now. She's gonna be mad.

"Louieeeee. Where are you, little scoundrel?" I thought about hiding and making her work for my affection but after what I just witnessed between the goblin boy and Hank in the garden, a thought crossed my mind that one day, this neurotic human will no longer be here to love me. Or maybe I won't be here for her to love. And who would she love without me? A human without a cat to dote on is the loneliest kind of human. So just this once, instead of making her work for my affection and prove her worthiness, I ran to her, and she collected me in her salt-sweaty arms.

"Louie! What are you doing all the way out here? You know you don't have any front claws and really don't have any business being outside. Honestly…" She kissed me several times too many, but I tolerated it for her sake.

"And who's this?" she asked. Oh right, the goblin boy.

"I'm Jimmy! I didn't mean to barge in. Your cat stole my bouncy ball, so I followed him back here to get it back, but then I saw…"

"What did you see?" Mae asked. She looked confused because looking around the garden, it was just the goblin boy, her, and me.

"Nah, never mind. You wouldn't believe me," he responded, clearly selling my human short.

"What if I told you, Jimmy, that I've seen some pretty crazy things back here and I *will* believe you. I trust you," Mae said. Honestly, sometimes this girl is just too nice.

"Really?" Jimmy asked. Mae nodded.

"I saw Hank. My dog that died last year."

Mae's eyes filled with tears. I wish they'd fall so I could lick their salty goodness from her cheeks. She doesn't like my "sandpaper tongue" though. Sigh.

"Jimmy, that's wonderful," Mae replied.

"So, you believe me?" he asked.

"Of course I do," Mae said gently. "This here is a magical garden, and I believe that you saw Hank. I'll tell you what. You can come here anytime you miss Hank and hang out with him. Would you like that?" Mae asked.

Jimmy nodded enthusiastically. "I would very much, ma'am."

"Please, it's Mae," she stuck her hand out to shake the boy's, annoyingly throwing me off balance in her arms. The two exchanged more words but I had tuned out by that point. That night, Mae cuddled me extra close while she fell asleep and even let me lay on her head, so I suppose it was a worthwhile encounter that day.

23

FLAME OR FORTUNE

Mae, 2022

The late summer heat in Cale Cove brought a drought like no other in history. The once vibrant, lush grass of the suburban yards was now yellow and brittle. It made its thirst known by producing a loud *crunch* when underfoot. If things were dry and dusty at the carnival, they'd only grown more arid in the days that followed. Mae initially kept up with watering the garden, but when the city of Cale Cove advised residents against watering for sake of water preservation, she watched the once-beautiful garden shrivel before her eyes. Even the pond's water level was so low that by the time it was ready to add the koi, there wasn't sufficient water anymore. Mae continued to pull weeds to keep some sort of maintenance going, but it broke her heart to see the vibrancy fade to the will of nature.

Mae was sitting on the porch with a glass of iced tea. She'd just finished dinner and was watching the golden sun change from yellow to pink just over the horizon line. Cale Cove had the most magnificent sunsets, she thought to herself. This time of day, the traffic had dispersed and the only presence around was the occasional walking couple and a few swallows chattering and flitting from tree to tree above. Mae had exchanged a few text messages with Miles, but largely, they hadn't talked about the night of the carnival or the morning after. It wasn't something that could be easily explained via text and anyway, Mae hated texting. There was too much subtext, too much to misinterpret when one is devoid of tone, inflection, and body language.

She rocked herself slowly on the chair with one leg pushing off the porch railing. Swirling the fast-melting ice in her glass, she gazed up into the trees in an overheated trance. In the distance, firecrackers sounded, followed by the squeal of children. What was it about summer that kids always seemed to have access to fireworks? Not even close to the fourth of July, yet fireworks always seemed to be present in the street around dusk.

Mae rocked herself into a pre-sleep, the kind where you lazily close your eyes but are still very much present to your surroundings, not yet having drifted off. Her head rested on the back of the chair and the steady, dry breeze played with her hair. More firecracker sounds. This time, the laughs were short-lived. The kids were probably called in by their parents, Mae figured. She rocked quietly for several more minutes until the sound of harried voices turned to frantic screams interrupted her lack of thought. She opened an eye and looked around, but didn't see anyone, so she settled back into her porch rhythm.

Then again, screams. This time they seemed closer, so Mae stood from her seat and walked to the edge of where her grass meets the sidewalk to look farther down the street in the direction from where the screams originated. Just then she saw it above the rooftops—smoke. Big, black, billowing smoke arising from two houses beyond. The wind pushed the smoke in her direction, and she headed to the backyard. Expecting to see fire two houses down, she was now faced with a backyard of blaze approaching the garden. The dried earth ushered in the fire so quickly it had now spanned three yards in a matter of moments. A panic rose in Mae's chest and her pulse pounded like an incessant bass drum in her ears. In the distance was the faint sound of sirens; thankfully, someone was coming.

Perhaps foolishly, Mae grabbed the garden hose and started it, trying in vain to tame the fire approaching her beloved backyard oasis, but before long a firefighter yelled behind her, "We've got this ma'am! Please back away to safety." She remembered the kids whose screams first alerted her to the chaos and after ditching the garden hose, ran toward their house. Two little boys were panicked and crying. She enveloped them into her arms and hugged them. She recognized the one from the garden with Louie and asked him where their parents were. The boys shouted, "They just went for a walk to the lake! They weren't supposed to be gone long."

"JIMMY!" screamed a frantic woman. Mae backed away as Jimmy's presumed mother gathered her crying son into her arms.

"What the hell happened?!" exclaimed a man Mae assumed was their father.

"I'm not sure. It might've been fireworks. Everything is so dry it just took off in no time," Mae said.

After calming the boys down and talking to their parents, Mae returned to her house, where the firefighters now had the blaze under control. She forced herself to take a few deep breaths to calm her racing heart, but the sight of the charred garden threatened the lump in her throat to break loose. Tears began to silently stream down her face as a single word escaped her lips, "No." She sank down to her knees seeing all that was no longer—the grape vines, the coneflowers, the endless rows of lettuce and snap peas were blackened to oblivion. Her connection to Lucy. Earl. Miles' mother. Hank. Gone.

Mae felt a warm hand between her shoulder blades and turned to see Miles next to her. She stood and he held her in an embrace. "Mae…I'm so sorry."

"The garden," was all she could make out between tears. Miles stroked Mae's back until she calmed, and they separated. She wiped her eyes with the palms of her hands and approached the backyard only when the firefighters advised it was safe to do so. She was numb to the conversation between them and Miles as she surveyed the damage. The fence surrounding the garden was charred. The only feature that made the garden feel as it had been present was the cement bench, still solidly poised at the edge. Mae remembered the first time she'd spoken to Lucy there and the countless conversations that had happened since. Lucy had been here to talk to her father. Patty to Earl. Miles to his mother. Jimmy to Hank. The garden that had brought so many people so much closure, joy, and understanding was now a hollow shadow of what it once was.

Patty joined Miles in the driveway looking silently upon the scorched yard, knowing what Miles was thinking, because she herself had thought it already. She draped an arm around his shoulder, and he turned to hug her, too. Cassie ran up the sidewalk as the firefighters were packing up their truck and she gasped, "What happened?! Is everybody OK? I just saw flames from the brewery window."

"Everybody's OK," Miles answered. "Luckily, it didn't touch any houses, just…"

"The garden," Cassie said solemnly. "Oh, Mae…" she found her friend at the edge of where the garden once thrived and squeezed her hand. "I'm so sorry. I know what this meant to you."

Mae nodded silently and rested her head on her friend's shoulder. In the driveway, more neighbors had gathered, asking each other what had happened, offering each other support, and lamenting the driest summer in Cale Cove history. They chattered about how lucky they were that the fire was contained to the yard and hadn't touched any houses. How lucky they were that the boys who made the innocent mistake of lighting fireworks in their parents' absence were OK. Lucky? Sure. Mae supposed they were quite unfortunate though, too.

❈❈❈❈❈❈

Mae wasn't sure how long it was until everyone filtered back into their homes and the fire department left. It could have been hours, or it could have been minutes. Her senses were clouded by the dissipating smoke and pit in her stomach that re-established itself every time she remembered what she'd lost. Cassie had returned to the brewery, citing the "capable hands" she was leaving Mae in, those of Miles. He spoke to the firefighters and joined Mae on the porch once everyone had left. She wasn't crying anymore, but her eyes were still red, and she was silent, standing and gripping the porch railing, staring out at nothing in particular. She dug one hand into the pocket of her shorts, searching for what she'd just discovered was no longer there. Lucy's locket must have slipped out of her pocket in the commotion of the night. Mae's heart, already heavy, sunk lower into her stomach.

"Mae, I'm so sorry, is there anything I can do?" Miles offered.

She sniffled and looked at him, "No, Miles. I'm sorry. The way you came over and Jared was just..."

"Don't," he said gently, "it's OK. I read all your texts. You say nothing happened and I trust you."

"He was a mess. I couldn't send him off to drive drunk. It was the only thing I could think to do, but I swear up and down that relationship is so beyond over," Mae let out a little laugh as she rubbed her eyes in exhaustion. "Honestly, Miles, it's almost comical how insane it was, and I'm not regretting leaving him for a single second."

Miles then smiled and said again, "I know. I trust you."

Miles sat back in the porch chair and watched while Mae leaned back onto the railing. They were quiet for a few moments, neither knowing what to say next nor minding the silence after the rush of the evening. Miles cleared his throat at one point and suggested, "We can replant. Nothing is ever really lost."

"We?" Mae asked.

"Yes, we," he replied with a grin.

Mae had a thought and shared, "I know it's kind of silly how attached I've gotten to the garden. It's not even mine… this house isn't even mine," she gestured around her, "but the garden was more than mine or yours. It was a little oasis. A connection to…you know…them." Suddenly Mae remembered the dream she had when she first arrived in Cale Cove of the people trying to talk to her, but she couldn't hear them. Of course. She now knew it was everyone who needed the garden revived. Everyone on the other side of the veil between this life and whatever lies beyond, waiting for their connection to their living loved ones to be reestablished. And now it was scorched. She had let them down.

Mae noticed an envelope on the floor of the porch that Miles had been holding when he arrived in the commotion of the fire earlier. She pointed at it and asked, "What's that?"

Miles grinned. "That," he said, "is what I was carrying to bring to Patty when I was walking by earlier and saw all the commotion. Mae could have been mistaken, but he had a mischievous glint in his eye as he explained this. Ah, perfect timing." His gaze shifted to an incoming visitor.

Patty was walking up the path to the house, carrying a pitcher of iced tea and a plate of cookies. She was grinning from ear to ear and said, "I heard there was some unfinished business over here that I needed to attend to."

Mae looked in confusion from Miles to Patty and back to Miles, searching for a clue to what was going on. "I'm lost," she said. "Unfinished business? What are you two up to?"

Patty placed the goodies on the porch table and instructed Mae, "You might want to sit down for this."

24

WHEN THE NIGHT IS OVER

Lucy, 1958

Her eyes filled with tears holding in what she could not say aloud as Lucy sat in her wedding dress, next to her dad on their bench in the garden. She'd be leaving soon to start her new life with Kurt and these secret garden meetups would be over. All of the hours she'd spent with her father in this backyard retreat, healing her heart, escaping the finality of death, would be gone, leaving her to face the harsh world's reality: her father was dead and had been for some time. Her hands bunched fistfuls of her dress while she held back emotion.

"What on your mind, kid?" John asked.

Lucy, almost startled that he was still there, swallowed hard and shook her head. She couldn't tell him, but she had to.

"Kurt," she started, then paused. Deep inhale. With a swift exhale, she strung her words together. "Kurt's job is taking us away from Cale Cove, dad. I have to leave." She couldn't bear to look at him. To see the disappointment in his face. "This has been so…indescribably wonderful. I don't know how I would have survived if you didn't start this garden, dad, if I didn't have it as a refuge to see you."

She looked at him then, his own eyes filled with tears and, what was it? Not quite sadness. Not disappointment. Compassion? Lucy was confused but continued. "It's the right thing to do. We kids are all mom has now and I need to set an example as the oldest. This will make her proud. If she was disappointed in me, I couldn't bear it." Her voice cracked at the last word, and she tried hard to hold the tears back, but they trickled down her perfectly blushed cheeks. She delicately wiped them away to preserve her makeup—the one rare time that she wore any.

John's eyes were warm and patient. "Luce…" he said. "This garden is great. And it *has* been wonderful this time we've had together."

"How can you be so calm about this?" she asked.

"Because it was never the garden that you needed. Sure, it gave you a place to set aside your worries and stress and focus on the task at hand, but you never needed it to talk to me. I'm always here, kiddo. I'm always with you. Every time you think of me, you can guarantee I feel it. I've never left you. Not for one day."

Lucy's shoulders caved as she sobbed, but this time they were happy tears. She watched her dad's serene face as he talked, and she had no choice but to trust him. Patty and her dad were the two people she trusted most in the world and if John was telling her the garden was effectively a convenient illusion, then she believed him. One question still lingered though.

"Why can't we hug? It's so hard missing your hugs, dad."

"Ah, come on. I was a reluctant hugger at best," he laughed at himself. "My body is still dead, Lucy, so we're separated by the physical part of reality. But the world is so much more than physical, don't you think? Every thought, every feeling your gut tells you is real. Those aren't physically tangible, are they?"

"No," Lucy agreed, "no, they're not." She paused to consider her next question. "So, I can still talk to you wherever I end up? Not in this garden…not in Cale Cove at all?"

"Always. Whenever, wherever," he confirmed.

"I just wish I could stay in the safety of this haven where nothing can touch us," Lucy lamented.

John carefully considered before replying, "Safety, my dear one, is in the presence of connection, and connection has no physical bounds."

25

REBIRTH

Mae, 2022

While a charred garden might seem entirely destructive and a loss worth mourning, burning at the end of a season does have notable benefits. It adds wood ash to the soil. Ash contains numerous trace minerals, which effectively replace those nutrients in the garden. Burning kills weed seeds, fungi, and other bacteria that are typically a nuisance to eradicate in a garden that you wish to remain free of chemicals, as is the case with growing vegetables. All of this, Mae learned from her optimistic Googling after the great garden fire toasted her masterpiece. She'd decided that because it was so late in the summer and nearly fall now, there was no use in attempting to replant the garden this year. She'd have to wait until next year and even then, had no idea where to start. Hence, her online research in all things garden burning. The websites and blogs she'd found had obviously *planned* their burning, but nonetheless, Mae was determined to make lemonade from lemons.

The night of the fire when Patty came to retrieve Miles' mysterious paperwork, they were both acting oddly until Miles gave Patty the go-ahead to let Mae in on the secret.

"It's hard for me to decide if I should cut right to the chase and fill in the details after or if I should give you some context first and then save the punchline," Patty explained.

"You guys are honestly kind of freaking me out right now. Is everything OK?" Mae asked.

Miles laughed and Patty smiled at Mae, "Everything is great, honey. Do you remember a few weeks ago when you were applying for jobs out on the porch, and I stopped by? You told me you were afraid to love Cale Cove as much as you do because you weren't even sure you could stay here. You were unrooted."

"Were? I think I still am," Mae replied.

"Not any longer, honey. Not if you want to be, anyway. The paperwork Miles was bringing me was from his father, who is an attorney. Lucy's attorney, to be more specific. Apparently, many moons ago, Lucy worked with Miles' father to draw up a will, in which she named me to be the executor of her estate."

"I thought you two hadn't talked in years," Mae confounded.

"We hadn't! I was just as surprised as anyone. Of course, there were no bad feelings there. It was just that life happened, and we never got back in touch. I first heard of her passing and the next day heard from Michael, Miles' dad," Patty explained. "The way that I understand how things happened is that after Lucy's own mother passed, Michael called Lucy back to town because she had been left her mother's entire estate, including this house. Lucy neither wanted to live in it nor sell it, so she kept it as a rental and didn't tell anyone. There were too many memories here for her. She'd lost her best friend—her daddy—here and left her childhood so abruptly behind when she married Kurt; it was all too much for her to want to come back to.

Her mother's passing inspired her to draft a will of her own, and working with Michael on that, she'd grown fond of the young lawyer. Knowing that she didn't want to sell the house, it was a perfect synchronicity that Michael's family was relatively new in town and looking for a place of their own. The wonderful Robertsons," Patty paused to squeeze Miles' hand, "moved into this house after Lucy's mother passed. That's how Miles grew up here."

"OK…I follow so far," Mae said. "I'm not sure where you're going with this though."

"Right! Get to the point, Patty." Patty drew in a long sip of iced tea and continued, "So, I was the executor of the estate, which included this house. The papers Miles was bringing me are the final paperwork and deed from his father for me to give you to you. You, Mae, are the person your grandmother wanted to have this home."

Mae's jaw instinctively dropped, and her brow furrowed. She was speechless and still very confused. She tried to ask a question, then closed her mouth when she couldn't form words. Then she tried again, "Lucy died three years ago. Why is this coming up now?"

"Your grandmother was a creative one, Mae," Patty said with a wink. "She wrote a letter to be given to me, as the executor, upon her death. She knew of the power of the garden, as you both are now familiar with. She wanted to ensure it stayed in her family but wasn't ready to tell them of a childhood she'd obscured from them. You were young at the time, Mae, I think just a baby, when she drafted her will. She loved you more than anything and knew you would be drawn here one day. She instructed me, via the letter, to wait until you were called to it, not to seek you out.

"Her estate paid for the maintenance of the house and Miles has kept it up since, waiting for someone we didn't even know to reclaim their place as its rightful owner. The day that you came to Cale Cove and marched up to this porch to inquire about renting, I had an inkling right away. Later, I let Miles in on the details of my task as executor and he confirmed your full name to me—from your rental agreement—and we both knew you were who Lucy called back home. Honestly, honey, we've been delinquent in getting things in order until now. Sorry about that."

Butterflies fluttered in Mae's chest as she struggled to find the right words to say. "This is mine?" was all she could manage. A tear brimmed in each eye as she thought about staying here, in this lovely home, in her newly-beloved Cale Cove even longer. Forever, if she wanted. This house was Lucy's. It was her past and her present. The mysterious and seemingly random way she found it was all Lucy. Her hand was at play in it all.

"It's yours, honey," Patty confirmed.

Mae pulled Patty into a tight hug and let her eyes leak with the overflow of happiness in her heart. She then hugged Miles and after they parted, stretched her arms across the porch railing, remembering the fun they'd had painting it this summer. Painting *her* porch. "I live here now!" she exclaimed.

Miles and Patty both laughed.

"Well, you already did…" Miles corrected.

"But I can stay! It feels like home because it *is* home," Mae remarked, one hand fondly over her heart.

※※※※※※

Mae still felt like she was floating a couple days after that porch conversation. She could simultaneously hardly believe it and absolutely believe it, given the synchronicity and feeling of comfort and ease she'd experienced since first appearing in this charming town. Mae of course knew she wanted to keep the house and stay, but she'd need to figure out a few things first. Namely, a job. It had been a wonderful summer of unemployment, living off of her severance while falling in love with Cale Cove, but autumn was around the corner, and with it, the dwindling end of her stipend. She'd been selective with the jobs she applied to at first, but now was throwing applications into the ether at an alarming rate, hoping something would stick.

Taking a break from the applications is when her mind and typing fingers wandered to a new browser tab to investigate what to do about the charred remnants of the garden behind her (*her!*) house. After reading a few articles, she ultimately decided she would not replant until spring, choosing to let the wood ash do its thing in boosting the nutrients or whatever it was doing. In a way, it was kind of beautiful to let the tragedy coincide with the innate cycle of nature: death to bring rebirth. Like everything in nature must die, so, too, would her garden. Only now she understood that just like Lucy's presence in the garden, nothing ever really dies. Death is merely a step in an ongoing, ever-present cycle of life.

After Patty and Miles had gone home the night of the fire, Mae feared that no longer having the garden to connect, she'd lose Lucy forever. Miles would lose his mother forever, and Patty Earl. The thought was almost too much to bear. She whispered in the quiet darkness of her bedroom, "Lucy, please don't let it be so."

"I told you sweetheart, I never left you and I never will," came Lucy's sing-song voice from the foot of Mae's bed. She strained her eyes in the dark, but Lucy was unmistakably there, and Mae felt as though her heart might burst from her chest.

"Lucy!" Mae exclaimed. "You have no idea how happy I am to see you. But how could you keep this whole 'your house is my house now' thing from me?!"

Lucy chuckled as she looked out the bedroom windows to the charred earth outside. "I thought you might ask that. It had to be you, Mae, the decision had to be you. I knew you'd be drawn here eventually and when you were, well, it was no longer my responsibility to take care of these earthly affairs. I had to wait on Patty."

Mae was grateful for Lucy's presence now, but it didn't erase the fear from her mind entirely. She asked, "If the garden let me see you initially, how can I see you now? How can we still talk?"

"Well, honey, think about that time when you kids were youngsters and we went to Florida on vacation. Remember how we played in the sand and built sandcastles all morning, just to have the tide come in and wash them away in the afternoon? My life in my body was like that sandcastle. What you saw it for washed away with death. But where did it really go? The sand is still there. The water is still there. It's just transformed. Our substance, our love still remains. The garden was merely an impetus for you to see the castle for the sand."

"So, the garden was just a tool? To get me in a sort of… mind space…where I was ready?"

"Precisely."

"The garden isn't magical at all?" Mae asked disappointedly.

"Well, I wouldn't say that necessarily. It did what it needed to do." Mae looked sad, and her grandmother read her mind, "Now don't give me that pout. You can and absolutely should replant it. Wouldn't it be selfish to keep a gift like this to yourself? The weight of grief is invisible but present all around us, weighing on people in ways we can't imagine. You were drawn here to resurrect," Lucy smiled at her choice of words, "this green space so that others can connect in the way you have."

"But why me? Why did you choose me?" Mae wondered.

"Your gifts, honeybee, lie in your ability to connect with people. You've always had the gift of gab and it's easy for you to draw people in, to know them, and to love them. This gift will bring others to the garden to heal in the way that you have. They trust you," Lucy explained.

Mae was honored. She nodded and reassured Lucy, "I understand. I'll revive it; don't worry."

"I'm not worried about a thing, darling."

26

IT GOES ON

Mae, Spring 2023

Mae's senses awoke simultaneously by the bright sunlight streaming through her east-facing bedroom windows and the clanging of pans in the kitchen below. She reached her hand over to the other side of the bed, now notably empty but warm to the touch. She slipped on a bathrobe and walked downstairs. The smell of freshly brewed coffee filled the air, along with the gentle sizzle of bacon.

"Good morning, sleeping beauty," Miles said as he handed her a cup of coffee. "They must be working you hard this week for you to sleep in this late."

Mae smiled at the scene: Miles with mussed hair making breakfast in the kitchen where he learned to cook with his mother, where Lucy learned to cook from her mother, and where Mae realized she was in love. "Nah, not too hard. Well, maybe. It's my own doing. Still so much to learn and I want to know all of it."

"For career's sake or for personal interest?" Miles asked.

Mae smirked, "Maybe a little of both." She was now working as a graphic designer for a national gardening magazine. The one, in fact, that published the book on

Midwest flowers she impulsively purchased at the Cale Cove market last year. Any acquired on-the-job knowledge now directly benefited her plans to rehab the garden. Because the magazine had offices and employees all over the country, she was able to work remotely from home. Miles had helped her convert a bedroom upstairs into an office, painting it a beautiful, deep turquoise.

She accented the walls with airy white curtains that had a geometric yellow border because they reminded her of a tablecloth Lucy used to have. Her desk faced the street so she could peep at her beloved town outside. Plenty of houseplants adorned the room, bringing the charm of the garden aesthetic inside, so she could feel connected even while working. While the painting of her office was much less eventful than that of the porch (namely, nobody ended up covered in paint), her office was now her second-most favorite part of the house, after the garden of course.

Today was Saturday, the long-awaited replanting day. After breakfast, the two dressed and started for the garden. Remarkably, there were tufts of green already peeking up through the soil. Mae felt reassured that the earth would heal, and her garden would bloom again. Once she reached the stanchion at the entrance of the garden, her eyes caught on something shiny, glinting in the sunlight. She approached it and noticed immediately it was her lost locket, Lucy's locket.

Her stomach floated to her throat as she clasped her fingers around it, pulling it into her chest. The metal was warm from the sunlight. Mae spun around looking for who had placed it there but saw only a sandhill crane at the rear of the lot, watching her. They stared at each other for a moment, then the crane bowed its head in a nod, and promptly flew away.

"Everything OK?" Miles said beside her.

"Everything's perfect," Mae replied, dangling the locket on its chain in front of her so that Miles could see.

His mouth opened in surprise, then closed in a knowing smile. One word escaped him, "Lucy."

"Lucy," Mae replied. She opened the locket to find a tiny photo of her younger self enveloped in Lucy's arms—a warm grandma hug.

Mae heard voices approaching behind them, toward the house, so she spun around and squinted against the sun. She brought her hand to her forehead to block the sun in order to see who was coming down the yard. Patty, Cassie, and Smitha walked next to each other, chatting and laughing as they traipsed. Patty was carrying her signature platter of lemon cookies and iced tea, and Cassie was pulling a wagon full of plants. Smitha carried the gloves, shovels, and a tiny rake.

Mae gasped in surprise, "What are you guys doing here?!"

"Oh, you didn't think you'd be reviving this little piece of heaven alone, did you?" Patty asked.

"Yeah girl, this is a shitload of work. Miles called in reinforcements. We got your back," Cassie added.

Mae could think of nothing better than whiling the day away in her favorite place with her favorite people. A little dirty, a little sweaty, but filled with lemon cookies and iced tea, and sustained by laughter. As the crew worked, Miles paused to put an arm around Mae and pull her into a hug. "Are you happy to have this piece of magic back?" he asked.

Mae looked around. Her cherished Cale Covians—Miles, Patty, Cassie, and Smitha—were hard at work in the garden around her, determined to return it to its former beauty. Louie was sunbathing belly up on the grass close by, lazily batting at a butterfly. It was a beautiful and sunny spring day in the town where she knew she always belonged. Her heart exploded with love at the thought of it all, that this simple, beautiful life was hers. That despite loss, grief, heartbreak, and best laid plans going awry, people are more resilient and open with their hearts than she previously understood. That broken hearts heal, hope rekindles, and connection is at the center of it all. She smiled at Miles, then tilted her head to rest on his shoulder and said, "The magic is life itself."

PATTY'S LEMON COOKIES

Ingredients

2 sticks butter, room temperature
1 1/2 cups granulated sugar
3 tablespoons lemon zest
3 tablespoons fresh lemon juice
1 egg
3 cups all-purpose flour
1 teaspoon baking soda
1/4 teaspoon salt
1/4 cup sugar, for rolling cookies

For glaze:
1 cup powdered sugar
2-3 tablespoons lemon juice

Directions
1. Preheat the oven to 350 degrees and grease a cookie sheet.
2. In a mixing bowl, beat butter, sugar, and lemon zest for 1-2 minutes.
3. Add the lemon juice and egg, beat to combine.
4. Gradually add in flour, baking soda, and salt, mixing until combined.
5. Form dough into balls, then roll each ball in sugar. Place a couple inches apart on cookie sheet. Bake 12-14 min or until the edges are slightly golden.
6. Allow cookies to cool a few minutes, then move to a cooling rack.
7. Prepare lemon glaze by mixing together powdered sugar and lemon juice in a bowl. Drizzle the cookies with desired amount of glaze.

PATTY'S MINT TEA

Ingredients

2 packed tablespoons of fresh mint leaves
4 cups water
Honey, to taste

Directions
1. Rinse mint leaves and place in a French press.
2. Bring 4 cups of water to a boil.
3. Pour boiling water over mint leaves and let steep for 10 minutes.
4. Press down the plunger of the French press and pour tea, adding honey to taste.
5. Drink entirely hot or leave mint leaves in French press and store in the refrigerator for a stronger flavored cold tea; serve over ice.

ACKNOWLEDGEMENTS

Writing a book is inherently vulnerable; it's sharing with the world pieces of the most intimate part of yourself: your thoughts. So first I'd like to thank you, reader, for choosing to spend your valuable time reading this pet project of mine. It truly is an honor.

I'd also like to extend my gratitude for those who inspired and supported the process of creating this book:

To dad, because without the joy of loving you and pain of losing you, I'd never have been privileged to know the beauty and strength that comes from moving through grief and the appreciation for the simple goodness of life.

To Tom, for offering endless support and assurance, being a soft place to land when grief is too much, and for being my biggest cheerleader in everything I do. I am deeply grateful you find me deserving of your love. (He is also the designer of the stunning cover of this book.)

To mom, for always encouraging the many expressions of my creativity and supporting me through many projects, even the ones that end in disaster.

To Kelly, for encouraging me to make a small habit of writing "just 20 minutes a day," which in turn produced this novel. Also for being the first to read the manuscript and offer honest feedback. I respect your praise as the highest, given that you read about 848493 books in a year.

To Kristin, for always being ready to talk about all things esoteric and life-giving and offering your unique perspective on such things.

To Eric, for being an enthusiastic early reader of the manuscript; your persistence broke me out of my bubble of comfort, thankfully to be caught by your ardent support.

To Emily and Amy who forever offer judgement-free conversation, friendship, idea incubation, and general inspiration for the kind of woman I aspire to be.

To my therapist, Debb, who through our work together gave me the concept of *akeru*—the space you create for new abundance when you have endings—which allowed me the mental space to write a novel.

To my wonderful editor, Michaela, who perhaps took on this project as a favor to a coworker/friend, but knocked it out of the park regardless.

To the people of the wonderful town in which I reside, you know you who are. More than you know, I appreciate your open-armed acceptance of me into the fold of your community and your readiness for sharing life, friendship, and many laughs over cold beers at our favorite spot.

ABOUT THE AUTHOR

Haley is a true Midwestern girl who spends her days writing for the corporate world and her free time daydreaming while running or paddle boarding on a nearby lake. The inspiration for her first novel was drawn in part from working through the grief of losing her father, contemplating career redirection after being laid off, and falling in love with all the charm, friendships, and quirky ways of the small town to which she recently moved. She lives in Wisconsin with her husband and their chubby orange cat.

Made in the USA
Las Vegas, NV
20 November 2023